SLOW WALK IN A SAD RAIN

SLOW WALK IN A SAD RAIN

JOHN P. McAFEE

WARNER BOOKS

A Time Warner Company

Warner Books, Inc., 1271 Avenue of the Americas, New York, NY 10020
W A Time Warner Company

Printed in the United States of America
First Printing: February 1993
10 9 8 7 6 5 4 3 2 1

Library of Congress Cataloging-in-Publication Data

McAfee, John P.
   Slow walk in a sad rain / John P. McAfee.
      p.   cm.
   ISBN 0–446–51642–2
   1. Vietnamese Conflict, 1961–1975—Fiction.   I. Title.
PS3563.C2645S57   1993
813'.54 — dc20   92–54100
                                                                        CIP

Book design by Giorgetta Bell McRee

Dedicated to Rick Boyer
writer, teacher, friend.

To all New Mexico Military Institute Alumni,
who served in Vietnam, and to all veterans,
living and dead, who paid the price.

Acknowledgments

Many thanks to the following people for helping me with this novel: Maj. William Rawls, United States Special Forces, Retired; John Creech, John McMichaels, Steve Black, Evan Bracken, and the graduate creative writing class at Western Carolina University; to J. David Kiser and Ann Fagan for help with the final draft and its printing; to Helen Rees and Rick Horgan for their professional insight; to my brother, Russell McAfee; to my wife and son, Jeannie and Lewis McAfee, who had to listen to my screams as I erased more than I wrote; finally, to Jimmy Buffet, whose songs got me through some rough times.

Author's Note

I am a teacher. I am a teacher because once, many years ago, I met a small boy and his grandfather in Laos. The meeting did not seem important at the time, but, like the Vietnam War, it has grown so important to me that I had to tell you. This is your story, too.

Fiction has been described as truth-and-a-half. So it is within these pages. I have seen most of these events. Those I haven't have been told by the old warriors, who talk of such things around poker games, over beers, or when they're alone and think no one is listening. These are secrets, forged in the hot fires of combat, pressed on the soul like a medal, and polished years later—still gleaming, still hurting.

I wasn't a good officer. At twenty-two, I shouldn't have been an officer at all, especially in Special Forces. But I did listen and learn from the senior non-commissioned officers, the E-7s and E-8s, who were the backbone of the Green Berets. Because I listened, they showed me how to survive.

So now I teach others what I learned once in a very green jungle a million miles from West Texas.

SLOW
WALK
IN A SAD
RAIN

They say war affects a man.
Don't believe it.
If he looks at dogwood white
Blossoming spring on mountains
And thinks of phosphorus marking
Rounds calibrating death;
If the peaceful bee sounds
Like a ricochetting bullet
Off concertina; if the bee-sought
Rose seems an open wound—
What of it?
The night will gauze them closed
And find the bee home.
But the man—
Sleeps fitfully,
Lost in a firefight
Between sun and moon,
Calling for help
Down petal trenches,
Trembling under the wife's
Helpless touch.
They say war affects a man;
Don't believe it.

Don't Look Behind the Curtain

In front of you and at the end of a dusty yellow dirt road is a large barbed-wire gate. From the gate to a large telephone pole runs a wire that keeps the heavy gate balanced. Directly beneath the place where the wire attaches itself to the pole is a sign. It reads, NORMAL IS A CYCLE ON A WASHING MACHINE.

There is a cowbell attached to the gate. Ring it and someone in the machine-gun bunker directly in front of you on the other side of the gate will cautiously peer over the burlap bags filled with sand and ask, "What do you want here?" That someone is Quiet Voice. He's always asking questions like that.

Don't shake the beer cans on either side of the gate—the ones hanging on the razor wire. They'll make a noise, too. They're filled with rocks, and if you shake them, Quiet Voice will shoot you, and then you won't be able to answer his questions.

See that elephant carcass out there in the middle of all that razor wire? It rang the beer cans and bought the farm. The only one who can stand the smell is Spec. 7 Thompson. He's got an experiment going on in the cavity of the left leg of the elephant. We don't want to know what it is. The leg twitches sometimes when Thompson pushes a button by the gate, and it scares the hell out of whoever is walking by at the time. He's got plans drawn up to run a pneumatic hose into the trunk, which he wants to fill with air so the trunk can wave hellos and good-byes to people entering and leaving our camp. Projects like this keep Spec. 7 Thompson sane.

Now that you've rung the bell, I'll open the gate. I have to be careful because it's booby-trapped now that it's almost dark. I'm in charge of the camp and I have to authorize anyone in or out. I apologize if my green-and-black tiger uniform frightens. My face is painted to match the outfit; that might frighten you, too. I hope so because I'm scared shitless of strangers.

Welcome to Emerald City. Follow me up this lonely wooden tower and look through the Starlight scope. It turns everything green. Below the tower and to the right is the mortar pit, a magical place. I can turn the handle on the phone up here and Shotgun, my team sergeant, will pick it up down there and give me illumination, H&I, or "fire for effect." Everything is a brighter green when that happens. You can tell how close the enemy is by the number of "increments," or powder charges, Shotgun leaves on the tail of the mortar rounds. Things get real interesting when he takes all but one of them off. When he does this, the round doesn't go very far, which is good, since the enemy isn't very far either.

I watch Shotgun curse and jerk off the little pack-ages of powder from the round and shove it into the tube. When the shells explode on contact with the ground, I look through the scope and see the attacking troops turn into fantastic creatures that fly and scream like winged monkeys. When that happens, I smile and scream back.

Shotgun likes that.

The mortar pit is in the shape of a keyhole. The shaft of the hole is a long trench lined with sandbags. The keyhole is the mortar pit itself, with the mortar mounted on its baseplate in the middle. Shells are in a little shelter close to the pit and right under this tower. Sometimes, when I look through the scope, I can see a rabbit looking at his watch disappearing into that keyhole.

I have to be real tired for that to happen.

Shotgun says if an incoming hits the tower, it will explode before hitting the mortar rounds.

That's comforting.

To get my mind off the possibility of an incoming proving Shotgun right, I gaze through the Starlight. It's a scope built by one of the American companies to give us eyes at night. But that's not why I use it. I use it to hold on to because I'm a long way from Texas.

I like to look past our Special Forces camp to the little village of Thanh Tri, which is about two hundred yards to the south. It reminds me of that town in the movie *Shane*, with its tin roofs and wooden sidewalks and the sea of mud in the middle of a very tiny main street. The town used to be made of thatched huts and roofs. We burnt those down a long time ago.

I look into those five or six homes lining the street, and they seem quiet. Small fires on the dirt floors illuminate the doorways, and an occasional farmer squats there and has a last-minute smoke before retiring for the evening. I pretend the villagers are munchkins.

Running alongside the village and parallel to the

west of our camp is the Vam Co Tay River, a small tributary that feeds into the mighty Mekong. It's the villagers' highway to market. They travel by boat downstream during the high tide, do their business, take naps, or "pok" time, during low tide, and return on the next high tide. The river is also our only way to escape.

If we're lucky, the enemy will hit during high tide.

If we're lucky...

Where the tributary meets the Mekong is Moc Hoa, a river city of about a thousand people. It's the location of the headquarters for all the A camps, like ours, scattered throughout the flat and swampy delta of South Vietnam. We call the Moc Hoa headquarters the B team. We're an A team, they're a B team. A lot of thought went into choosing those names.

The A team is run by a captain.

That's me.

The B team is run by a colonel.

That's dangerous.

If you want to know what the delta is like, go to your nearest swamp and stand in it.

Until your socks rot.

And your underwear hangs in mud-stained rags from your crotch.

They grow rice in the delta.

Good choice.

Forty miles south of Moc Hoa and the Mekong is Can Tho, largest city in the delta and its ancient provincial capital. It is also the disembarking point for all Special Forces soldiers assigned to Company D, Fifth Special Forces Group, Airborne.

A team, B team and Company D.

Don't ask about where *c* went. Company D is the *c*.

Army logic.

That's where the tornado disguised as an old C-130 troop transport airplane set down all the young men it had snatched up in its destructive path across America. I was one of those men.

We've got all night up here. Sit down on this old gasoline can and I'll tell you what it felt like coming into country.

The plane dipped quickly and the old sergeant gave a nervous smile. We clutched our webbed seats and closed our eyes. It was our first lesson: hide the fear behind the smile.

Below, in darkness, starlight reflected brightly on the South China Sea. Above the wing the same stars shimmered with equal brilliance. Here, at that moment, we were close to heaven. Some of us were young schoolboys fresh from the classrooms; some, young toughs fresh from the streets; and all of us gripped our seats. Here, we were also close to hell.

To the left of our plane lay Can Tho, waiting for the next army to battle itself. Over Can Tho's roads drove Hondas, an occasional Citroën; and beside the roads walked all those people whom I never knew or understood.

In front of our plane lay Vinh Long. But it's small and all I remember of it is a dance one night for some Vietnamese official and how the paper lamps matched the stars reflecting in the great Mekong tributary, Hau Giang, which flows between Can Tho and Vinh Long. It was one of the few moments of beauty I experienced in Vietnam, and that's why I remember Vinh Long.

To the right stretched rice paddies, swamps, and a few forests. In the rice paddies were water buffaloes, mist, bugs, and night; leeches, hot sun, and silent peasants. Here and there, there were huts with palm roofs, an occasional mad hermit, foxholes, unnamed small, deep rivers, thick shoe-stealing mud, and death.

Otherwise, nothing important.

But it's the smell of the Hau Giang, large cousin to the Mekong, that I remember. It's the smell all great rivers have: of fish, oil, food, peels, animal blood, bodies with hands tied behind their backs, human excrement, beer and wine, dirt from Cambodian flatlands, and twisted tree trunks from the great mountains in the distance.

The Hau Giang smelled of all those things.

It smelled of the mess human beings can make.

Not a single stench that exists in the whole world is left out of it.

Smells of life and death, of home, lost loves, revived hatreds, and the unpackaged, unadvertised vibrant world.

Our plane was one of many scratching themselves free of human infestation, with low-flying helicopters punctuating the heartbeat of all of us who stepped off.

Those planes were full of courage landing along that Mekong tributary: haughty above the little sampans, arrogant above the little boathouses, proud and complex.

But occasionally, there are times . . . and they lie in the memory as dry and gray as a drained rice paddy, across the age-old and ever-young Hau Giang. These times talk about bravery, strength, happiness, sorrow, and how young men should have stayed on the plane instead of ending up lost on a strange, magical, and horrifying voyage.

Color those times brown.

Like the sampan that brought all of us—Quiet

Voice, Spec. 7 Thompson, and me—to Special Forces A Camp 134, located twenty miles above Moc Hoa and less than a mile from Cambodia.

Waiting for us was Shotgun. No one knew how long he had been in Vietnam or how long he had been waiting for us at the A Camp. He would show us how to survive.

The Opening Curtain

According to scientists, the triangle is the only shape in nature that does not occur naturally. So we didn't live inside a triangle.

We lived inside three of them.

The first triangle was a quarter mile of razor wire. The second triangle was located inside the outer wire and consisted of three huge earthen mounds ten feet high and four hundred feet long. These were called *bermes* by the French. From the air it looked like a crazed, giant mole hadn't been able to make up its mind where to go. At each corner of the berms were machine-gun bunkers facing outward, scanning the wire, looking for giant moles and things much worse.

In the middle of the wire and earthen triangles was a triangle made from old Conexes full of sand. A Conex is a steel packing crate the American armed services used to ship supplies to stranded bases around the world. Since there was no landing strip, we certainly qualified as stranded. Our Conexes had a lot of dents in them having been shoved out of the rear cargo doors of airplanes that flew low and quickly by. Even if there had been a runway, planes wouldn't stop. Shotgun said they were chicken shits. We envied their cowardice. It gave us faith that someone had common sense.

Someone without appreciation for the damage a B-40 rocket can inflict when fired at close range had ordered a runway to be built outside the wire triangle. The rusted and twisted hulks of airplanes spoke eloquently as to the lack of interest that had led to the runway project's death. Landing an airplane at our sniper-encircled camp would be like attempting suicide in a government-made coffin and it was apparent that many such suicide attempts had been successful.

Had there been a working runway, we might have been tempted to run away from "home."

Our "home" sat in the middle of the sand-filled Conex triangle half-above and half-below ground. It was a long rectangular wooden shack with a tin roof covered with sandbags to absorb the occasional steel rain from incoming rockets and mortars, an unusual feature of the weather above the triangles.

The difference between steel rain and regular rain was that one went pitter-patter on the tin roof.

The other made your heart do that.

The wood of the building had long since turned a dusty brown and matched exactly the burlap color of the sandbags.

Five narrow steps led down to a front door made from steel and pieced together in fragments. Behind each fragment on the inside, Spec. 7 Thompson had rigged C-4 charges with blasting caps to blow the door outward in large steel chunks. When someone came to ring the doorbell, we'd set the charges off and the door would blow outward, fragmenting itself and any bodies in front of it.

We didn't have a lot of visitors.

It wasn't a normal home.

In the middle of our bunker were five more steps leading down to communications. One of us was always down there, connected by earphones to an electronic umbilical cord that was our salvation and our undoing. Besides the radio, the commo room had file cabinets, guns, procedure manuals, guns, a desk, more guns, and thermite grenades on top of everything. The idea of the thermite grenades was to burn and blow everything up, including us, in case the other team scored. We hadn't used it—not yet.

A family tradition.

The Addams family.

Members of the Hoa Haos, our mercenaries, were part of the family. We kept them on the outward triangle as our first line of defense. The Hoa Haos members and their families would huddle in cement bunkers covered by the thick dirt of the berms, peering through gun slots at the wire every night. You pronounce their name like this: *wah-how?* The question mark conveys the proper meaning.

We kept our "mercs" out there because they would slow down any assault with their bodies, and that would buy us time.

We let them have their families because they fought the other team harder if they knew their children might buy the farm along with them. Women and children would buy us time, too.

We encouraged family togetherness.

We huddled inside our triangle watching the ce-

ment bunkers just in case some of those mercenaries
might be playing for the other team.

Mercenaries are funny like that.

The Hoa Haos was a militant Buddhist sect of
Vietnamese and Cambodians who believed the best way
to get closer to the Buddha was to die fighting.

That fit with our philosophy quite well.

That's why we hired and trained them.

The reason why we watched them was because
their religious beliefs did not stipulate who they had to
fight to get closer to the Buddha.

The other team had a first and second string. First
string was the NVA, crack troops who'd learned under
the Vietminh fighting the French. They were fine-tuning
those lessons on us. The second string was the VC, the
Vietcong, South Vietnamese Communists who wanted
the two countries joined. They expected a nice job
afterwards for helping the first string. They'd never
played pro ball before. It's a cutthroat business.

If mortar shells had eyes, they would have noticed
the little yellow glows at night in the middle of the
barbed wire. The glow was phosphorescent paint on
claymores.

The claymores were wedge shaped, like pieces of
pie, and you pointed the fat end in the direction in
which you wanted them to explode. They were electron-
ically detonated antipersonnel mines. That means they
were giant shotgun shells that blew the shit right out of
several human beings at one time.

No shit.

They stood on tripods in the wire, facing out. They
were originally painted a dull army gray or green,
depending on what company got the contract to make
them.

Change number one: The other team turned them around and attacked on dark, moonless nights.

It's hard to see dull gray or green on dark, moonless nights. It's hard to see anything on dark, moonless nights. So when the attack occurred, those on the berm would set off the turned-around claymores and kill themselves. Problem here.

Change number two: We painted the backs of the claymores with phosphorescent yellow paint. When that yellow turned at night, those inside the triangle knew the other team was going to kill them, so they set off the claymores and obliterated everyone in the wire. Problem solved.

Change number three: The other team matched the paint, carried it into the wire, and painted the unpainted front of each claymore with phosphorescent yellow paint, making the whole claymore a bright yellow. They would then turn the claymore around again and attack. Those on the berm would note the color and set off the claymore, thinking it was still the other way around, and kill themselves again. Problem.

Change number four: Those still living inside the triangles painted new claymores on both sides and stuck them into the wire but first reversed the plates so what was front was really back and what was back was really front.

The other team, crawling through the wire, saw that the claymores were already turned, and attacked. Those inside the triangle set off the claymores and killed everyone in the wire again. Problem solved again.

Change number five: Because the war went on so long, both sides forgot which way the claymores were supposed to point. New people kept arriving due to the team draft, so no one used the claymores for fear of hurting the wrong person. The claymores just sat there like glowing ceramic crabs, frozen in an attack position. Their glow on the elephant's carcass was a comforting sight to those who peered from their bunkers.

Now, I know what you're thinking: elephant carcasses aren't the best reflectors of light. And you're right. The other drawback is that they smell bad for a long time. Our next-door neighbors, the gentle people of Thanh Tri, harped about this constantly, punctuating their displeasure with occasional sniper fire and booby traps.

You'd think they'd never smelled a dead elephant before. It wasn't as bad as the thirteen bodies we left in the wire during the dry season. Hell, you could smell them from a chopper at two thousand feet. The village didn't complain then. They cried a lot because some of the bodies were relatives.

But they didn't complain.

Or go near the wire to get them.

The wire was strong enough to hold a lot more dead bodies.

American made.

Was it our fault the wind blew from Cambodia through camp and into their village? Besides, where in the Special Forces operations manuals *FM 31-32* and *FM 31-32A* is an elephant in the wire covered?

Personally, I think the villagers were mad because the NVA's showing up out of the blue with a male elephant meant their elephant, a female, could get pregnant. They needed a new elephant and we thwarted their plan. The old female in Thanh Tri could smell the young male in Cambodia and would trumpet sweet nothings and he'd answer with a quiet lover's rumblings every night. Elephants in love do not recognize national boundaries.

Are you confused? Let me back up and start at the

beginning of the elephant problems. That's when our luck started going bad, anyway.

That night, Christmas of '69, we watched the large truck roll to a stop in Cambodia as we'd always done, the glow of the taillights shining as the brakes were applied. We heard the tailgate slam down and the truck springs groan as the third-world bulldozer walked off the flatbed. The red taillights on the truck were the only Christmas lights we had.

We'd watched these lights nightly as the North Vietnamese continued stocking supplies for their next offensive.

Which was usually against us.

"What is it this time?" asked Quiet Voice, who only asked questions. Otherwise, he never talked.

One time I asked him, "Why do you always ask questions?"

And he answered, "How else am I supposed to make sense out of any of this?"

We tolerated his questions because he was our medic. His questions—"Where are you hit?" or "Does this help?"—were needed then.

Quiet Voice was a tall, gangly fellow, the kind who plays a good solid game of basketball in the eighth grade then quits high school in his junior year and does shift work. The war laid him off but he still had to eat. So he joined Special Forces and they taught him how to bandage wounds and raise puppies. That's when he started asking questions.

"Why am I raising this dog?"

And the medic-school personnel kept telling him, "You'll see."

And he did. On the final week of medical training at Fort Sam Houston, they took his grown puppy, shot it through the stomach and told him to save it if he expected to graduate.

He did.

"What happens to my dog now?" he asked.

"You won't need him where you're going," they answered, and promptly put the saved dog to sleep.

Quiet Voice had asked a lot of questions since then.

Watching on the berm that night with Quiet Voice was Spec. 7 Thompson. Only he wasn't really a specialist seven. There was no such thing as a specialist seventh class. Most of the specialists were fours, maybe one or two were fives. So Spec. 7 Thompson wasn't really a specialist seventh class.

You'll find that out later.

What he was was scary. You've met him before: that pimply faced teenager who invites you up to his room to show you how he's wired the door with a sixty-thousand volt current to kill his parents; the kid who rigged the headlight on his ten-speed to fire sharp pencils into anyone stupid enough to try to steal it. Spec. 7 Thompson stayed up late at night arguing sound-wave weapons technology when nobody else was in the room.

"If I only had enough coaxial cable, I could put a remote over there and see what's going on," Spec. 7 Thompson said, making his usual clucking sounds with his breath, which he did when frustrated.

"Knock off the fucking noise." That would be Shotgun.

Which is why we became quiet, wondering why the NVA needed an elephant and why some idiot would order an elephant to be brought by truck from the north. It wasn't comforting to know that the other team had senior officers like ours.

It was terrifying.

We spent our time being bored or being terrified. There was no in-between. During our bored time, we followed orders written by rational bureaucrats who worked rational hours and filed things rationally, such as:

"Silence must be maintained between the hours of 7:00 P.M. and 5:00 A.M. nightly in order to maintain silence.

"Remember correct radio procedure. The enemy is always listening. Do not use the radio when the enemy is near. Use only for emergencies.

"The following villages are pacified. Please sleep in the villages to ascertain if said villages are pacified. Report immediately if information is incorrect."

Those orders were for security reasons.

Secure was not a recognized feeling at our camp.

Two nights after that North Vietnamese elephant showed up, the two pachyderms broke our security. Since elephants can't read, they weren't aware of orders. They decided to meet outside of the village and inside the wire triangle around the camp.

If you're a male and you want to feel inadequate, just watch two elephants fuck.

It's like putting a sex manual on a billboard.

It's like putting a baseball bat in a washtub.

Their humping began to screw up our wire, which was needed for other security breaks. There were a lot of security breaks between 7:00 P.M. and 5:00 A.M. Elephants weren't the only ones who could not tolerate rules, no matter how rational.

We were standing there watching when Shotgun decided he'd seen enough.

"That's enough," he said. "I put a lot of time in that wire."

And over the berm he went. How he kept from tripping over the wire or cutting himself I don't know. He walked up behind the male elephant mounted on the female, pulled the pin on the grenade, grabbed the tail, hoisted himself up via the elephant's leg, and shoved the grenade up its ass.

There was a loud groan of pleasure from the elephant.

That was before the grenade went off.

The elephant died with a smile. The female trampled more wire and a couple of village huts. We took sniper fire from the female elephant's owners. We also took mortar fire.

Nobody likes to be awakened by the *1812* Overture without the music.

We left the elephant as a warning to other elephants. That's what you're supposed to do with dead bodies. Watch them glow yellow from the claymores night after night.

The mortar shells? They were coming from a part of Cambodia called the Parrot's Beak. It was called that because, on maps, a part of Cambodia projected sharply into Vietnam. To some colonels, the projection looked like a parrot's beak. To everyone else it looked like a big dick. But they couldn't call the area the Big Dick in staff meetings, so they called it Parrot's Beak.

Flowing out of the Parrot's Beak was the beginning of the Vam Co Tay River. From the air it looked like a string connecting the two countries. The stream divided just before it got to our camp. From the air it looked like a noose.

In 1969 everything in the village was the same as it had been in 1939; mortar shells were still coming out of Cambodia; villagers went to market in the province capital, Moc Hoa, during high tide and waited till the next high tide to go home; the rice was planted and harvested the same as it always had been. The three triangles north of the village were all that was different.

The triangles were A Camp 134.

The villagers knew that if they ignored the triangles long enough, the triangles would go away.

They were right.

Shotgun

Shotgun was filing the fuses on the grenades again. He was helpful like that, even when we didn't want him to be helpful. Of course, nobody had enough balls to tell Shotgun to leave things alone.

The problem was that you didn't know how far he'd file the fuses. There you'd be, in the middle of a world of shit, and the only way out would be a couple of strategically placed—okay, hastily lobbed—grenades, and you didn't have time once the pin was pulled to pick out where the grenades were supposed to go, lobbingly speaking.

One trick we used was to throw the grenades without pulling the pins. At first the other team would laugh at our rookie mistake. Then, they'd pick up the grenades and pull the pins to throw the explosive little baseballs back at us.

Boom!

It's hard to pitch with no arms.

Can't be done.

But they soon realized their mistake and began pulling the grenade pins out halfway and leaving the grenades on the ground. One of the many regulations issued to us by rational bureaucrats required us to "leave nothing behind the enemy could use." Thus we had to pick up our own grenades, and the pins fell out, which spoiled our day.

But grenade throwing is not what this is all about. It's about Shotgun.

"Shotgun, if you file those fuses too short, then you won't have enough time to pull the pin, get into a grenade thrower's stance, and throw the grenade." The grenade thrower's stance, as taught at Fort Benning, is this: one kneels on the left knee, right leg straight out behind the body as a brace, right arm cocked, grenade in hand. Of course nobody in their right mind would throw a grenade like that.

Shotgun chuckled at my little joke. "Neither will they," he said, clutching, like a hen with her eggs, the little rounded balls of steel to his massive chest, his eyes glowing with the vision of *the Cong* with no arms.

Since he always chose to file those grenades in the middle of the four-deuce mortar pit, surrounded by tons of explosives, I kept the conversation real short.

He slept in that mortar pit with his arm around the mortar barrel like it was an old dog. As captain of the camp, I was reminded by my superiors that his behavior was odd—whenever they remembered to inspect our camp. Daily shellings of our perimeter kept the inspections to a minimum.

I would point out to the infrequent inspectors, as we sprinted towards the bunkers to avoid whizzing pieces of communist shrapnel, that Shotgun's sleeping

with the mortar, while odd, did allow said mortar to
come on line quickly and silence those whizzing pieces
of shrapnel. The inspectors, huddled in the bunkers,
would agree on Shotgun's competency, but once safe
back at headquarters, they would forget. His odd behavior, therefore, had resulted in four silver stars and two
hearings for a Section Eight: mental aberration.

But Shotgun wasn't crazy. Hell, you could sit
down with him, slowly move his shotgun across the
table, and have a beer with him anytime. He'd sit there
with his case of Vietnamese beer and you with your
glass and he'd listen to anything you had to say. The
problem was that after Shotgun had had a few beers you
had to hold up your end of the conversation, which was
the only end. If you slowed down any, his hand would
wander slowly towards the shotgun. Since we were all
young, our reaction time gave us plenty of margin to
realize that conversation was lagging.

The Teamhouse was a whorehouse-bar-laundry we'd
built in Can Tho, the largest city in the delta, to
supplement our meager combat pay. Like cowboys, we
came to Can Tho only on the weekends, when we'd
have a drink and collect our profits.

It wasn't unusual for all kinds of military personnel
to visit the Teamhouse. We had crap tables for gambling, decent whiskey stolen or traded from various
officers' clubs in Can Tho, and a Filipino cook who
knew barbecue. Unfortunately, his taste in meat ran to
rats, not pigs. Still, we didn't have rodent problems in
our club, and meat costs were minimal. The Vietnamese
businessmen around us would also profit because they'd
bring rats to the cook when we had large crowds, thus
eradicating a potential health problem. At least that's
what the commendation said. (We received a commendation for being in charge of the project.)

"For improving the morale of the individuals in our indigenous forces and eliminating a potential health hazard by teaching existing businesses how to capture and eradicate a growing rodent problem, Special Forces A Camp 134 is hereby commended for a job well done."

We didn't eat there.

Our customers did.

We used the psychological-warfare funds for the building of the Teamhouse. The funds had been allocated to us to improve morale. Our mercenaries' morale was improved because we paid them to build the building. Our morale was improved because our combat pay was enhanced and we got free booze. We called our project OMCE, or Overt Mission for Capitalistic Enterprise. We sent pictures of our busy workers to *Stars and Stripes*, the army newspaper, but they wouldn't print it. John Wayne doesn't run gin mills, I guess.

Once, at the Teamhouse, a nonairborne soldier, commonly called a straight-leg, sat down at our table. Naturally, he had to be drunk out of his mind to do this, but his courage impressed us, nevertheless. Conversation in the bar stopped.

Then he fucked up.

"What are your hands shaking for?" he asked Shotgun.

We all froze.

"Are my hands shaking?" Shotgun asked all of us at the table.

"Hell, no, Shotgun," I said, smiling and leaning forward while taking the strap off my "Chicom" pistol. I called it that because it had been taken off a dead Chinese communist officer who'd been stupid enough to try and help the North Vietnamese. I wondered if the

pistols they took off the dead American officers were
called Amcaps, for "American capitalist."

Shotgun's hand was reaching for the shotgun.

"Your hands are a little blurry, Shotgun," I said,
"but definitely not shaking."

"Then why is the front of my shirt wet?" Shotgun,
feeling the front of his fatigues, seemed concerned.

"Don't you think it's hot in here, guys?" asked
Quiet Voice. "Haven't we all sweated a lot?" he said,
quickly pouring beer down the front of his fatigues.

We followed Quiet Voice's example.

By that time Shotgun had focused on our fatigues
and relaxed, with that flat, thin grimace he used as a
smile. Our reaction time hit a peak that day.

I slugged the kid at about the same time Quiet
Voice did, so it was hard to say who knocked him cold.
Both of us saved his life.

"Fucking leg," I said, kicking his body under the
next table.

Shotgun looked at the prone body and his mouth
got thinner. A crisis had passed.

We didn't have a lot of trouble at the Teamhouse.
We just let it be known it was Shotgun's drinking hole,
and things ran real smooth. We were surprised how
quickly the Vietnamese figured out how to make a profit
off our little demonstration of capitalistic enterprise.
There were a lot of T-shirts running around with the
words I SURVIVED SHOTGUN'S. They were clever people.
It wasn't their fault they lived in Vietnam.

Then, Colonel Black—just like the elephants—had
to come along and fuck everything up. He was the
colonel of the B team in Moc Hoa. He was always
passing along orders to his A team. Judging by his
orders, we'd concluded he was crazy.

He didn't look crazy. He was tall and handsome,

with thick hair and an air about him that said Princeton. We'd forgotten Princeton was the university that thought up the atom bomb.

He had this dream. Actually, what he described to us was a nightmare: a mobile four-deuce mortar unit. Since the baseplate of the 4.2 weighs as much as the fat lady in the opera, you can understand our concern with the term "mobile." Add the long tube, sight group, shells, and powder charges and you have a real problem. Naturally, this was pointed out to the colonel when he suggested this idea to us at the Teamhouse.

Since he was into us for ten g's from the crap table, we thought he was joking, trying to soften us up to let him off the hook. We—all of us but Shotgun— laughed our asses off. Shotgun was busy on his second case of beer at the time.

Colonel Black said he would send our trained Hoa Haos mercenaries with us for protection. The Hoa Haos belief was, you remember, that the only way to get to Buddha was to die in combat.

There were other ways, believe me.

Just ask Shotgun.

"Men . . ." Colonel Black always began his speeches that way. I don't know if it was to remind him or us. "Men, don't worry. My concept of a mobile rifle unit will provide ground support by laying down covering fire while you set up the mobile mortar unit to provide covering fire to the mobile rifle unit."

A mobile Möbius strip.

I told you he was crazy.

Later we found out that he'd been under a lot of pressure to do something with the new personnel sensors developed by Hughes Aircraft Corporation. They'd arrived one day on a chopper in a box marked "Top Secret—Personnel Sensors." We piled it with the other "top secret" boxes and went on with trying to stay alive. But somebody back in the world needed to know if they worked, and tightened the screws on the colonel. "Screw" is a term used often on field personnel.

Laughing at Colonel Black's sense of humor, we gave him a marker excusing a thousand dollars from his gambling debt, then stood up. We wanted to get back to camp before nighttime. We didn't have the night concession in Vietnam and it usually got nasty during those hours. Call it a turf battle.

Anyway, we thought it was neat how Colonel Black, explaining his idea, kept a serious face as we began filing past him to our jeeps outside. Then we noticed that Shotgun hadn't moved at all. This wasn't unusual. After two cases of Vietnamese beer, sometimes he didn't move for days, but we were embarrassed for Shotgun in front of the colonel.

As we put our hands tentatively under his arms to lift him Shotgun spoke. "Let's do the mission. I'm bored."

We sat back down.

The colonel outlined his plan.

The 4.2
Mobile Unit,
Part I

They're dog turds!" said Spec. 7 Thompson. Now, I know what you're thinking—there are no Spec. 7's in the army—and you're right. But Thompson had given himself the promotions every four months in-country as a way of marking time and not forgetting it. He'd paint the little upside-down chevrons under his specialist insignia on his sleeve, and then if he forgot how long he'd been in Vietnam, he'd look at his sleeve and count the chevrons and relax again.

We all celebrated the quarterly promotions by having a barbecue—elephant steak was a favorite—and toasting Thompson as he painted another stripe on his uniform. Life was good.

And they were dog turds. I checked the box again just to make sure we'd received the right one. "Top Secret—Personnel Sensors." We had. At moments like these I became nervous. I was always nervous with command decisions around Shotgun. Fortunately for me, he was over in the mortar pit talking to the mortar, explaining the upcoming vacation.

I put on my best command face. "Guys, these are sensors."

They all relaxed then and helped Thompson grab the plastic bag filled with dog turds and began pulling them from the crate.

"Why are these dog turds so heavy?" said Thompson.

With a great deal of effort we pulled the plastic bag free of its container. Naturally, the bag broke, spilling the contents. The sensors were coated with a good inch of turd-colored rubber. A little piece of metal could be seen in the center. Otherwise, each individual turd reminded me of the plastic puke we used to buy as kids from those joke houses. It would be neat to leave one of these in someone's chair just as they were about to sit down.

In the bottom of the box was a book of instructions and a monitoring machine. The book said the rubber was developed by California Specialty Products, Inc. Spec. 7 Thompson pointed out that his dildo had been made by the same company. Big deal.

The monitor came with a cord to plug into an outlet. Since electricity was nonexistent at Thanh Tri, we were a little concerned about whether or not it would work. But Thompson, excited at his new toy, fixed us up.

He walked out of the bunker across the area between triangles and grabbed the generator-attached TV cable from our South Vietnamese counterparts, who theoretically were supposed to mirror our every action when we were in combat. We had never seen them. They arrived one night in a helicopter, went inside their hootch, and never came out.

Someone in the State Department had decided that every A team should have a South Vietnamese equivalent to mirror every individual and every action of the A team. However, once the Vietnamese saw the type of missions our A team undertook, they went inside their hootch and never came out again except on payroll day, when they had to pay our Hoa Haos friends with the money we brought upriver weekly. The reason we brought the money upriver was that the first time we asked our Vietnamese counterparts to bring it, they took it downriver and never came back.

We wondered what they did inside their bunker besides watch television. Why television? The United States Agency for Internal Development had given them an electrical generator and television set for...for...for development, I guess.

Thompson came back carrying the cable, little sparks shooting from its end where he'd ripped it out of the hootch, and, with a little tinkering, attached an outlet to it and plugged in the monitor. It worked immediately. That's why Thompson deserved to be a Spec. 7.

Leave it to Quiet Voice to point out the problems.

"You guys seen a lot of dogs around here lately?" We shook our heads. "Do you know why?"

Sure we knew why. One of our Hoa Haos helpers favorite foods was dog soup. We found this out when we gave them German shepherds trained as watch dogs for the berms. Only one survived, and it had a psychopathic hatred of the Hoa Haos. We'd keep it inside until night, then release it. The dog kept the Hoa Haos gang in their bunkers. They didn't dare go out. We called the dog Pecker, since it spent its days licking that particular area.

"Won't this shit look a little weird, since there are

no dogs or wolves or foxes or anything else that shits turds like this left in Vietnam?'' Quiet Voice asked. He gave the little turds a shake.

Then he added in that little, still voice that always chilled us, ''Who's going to put the turds out in the field?''

A fact is a fact. Quiet Voice had definitely voiced a fact. Still, the sensors had to be placed over our area of operation (AO), which was a little smaller than Missouri, since it extended into Cambodia. Judging from the number of little rubber turds there were in the sacks, we had enough to cover the area. Things weren't that bad.

Then we heard Shotgun's voice over in the mortar pit; he was arguing with his mortar. ''What do you mean this mission isn't a good idea, that we're all going to die?''

His voice rose another notch. ''You're a goddamn coward!''

Things were that bad.

The 4.2 Mobile Unit, Part II

As I walked out of the camp carrying the sack of turds I glanced back at our sign on the telephone pole: NORMAL IS A CYCLE ON A WASHING MACHINE.

Shotgun had put the sign on the pole after a jeep full of inspectors had been blown up, not by a stray enemy round (it had been broad daylight), but by one of the inspectors. He (the inspector) had hooked the ring on the pin of his grenade to the door latch on the jeep. When he stepped out, the ring pulled free and off flew the handle. We knew it was an accident because he screamed for help. Spec. 7 Thompson pointed out that it would have taken the inspector ten seconds to pull the grenade off his belt.

That was five seconds too long.

We left the burnt jeep as a safety reminder. Grenades can kill if you don't handle them right.

I thought about our motto and the jeep as I was

circling at three thousand feet in a night-duty helicopter, dropping dog turds into the night. One ''bughead'' was flying the machine and the other was keeping a weapon trained on me as I reached inside a plastic bag, grabbed what looked to be a pile of dog turds, and threw them out the door. I guess they were resentful: they had to put their lives on the line for a sack of shit.

We called the pilots bugheads because they wore those army football helmets that had radio equipment inside so they could ask for help—or scream or cry—and their passengers couldn't hear them. In addition the army had added a visor that snapped down over their faces, allowing them to see out, while preventing passengers from seeing in. They looked like giant bugs with one huge reflecting eye. When they crashed, thanks to the helmet, their heads were always left intact. Small consolation to the rest of the body, but I must admit that as I fingered my soft jungle hat I did envy the fact that someone back home would recognize them when they died.

The night-duty helicopter was another idea of Colonel Black's. As a commander of the B team, he gave orders to the commanders of the A team. The night-duty order was pure Black. The commanding officers of an A camp were to take turns at being night-duty helicopter commander, rotating weekly. We were to fly around our area of operation with a large jet-landing light hooked up to the bottom of the helicopter to sweep the ground and allow us to spot the enemy, who, theoretically, would freeze like a possum caught in the light while we ran over him with our superior technology.

It didn't quite work that way.

The B-40 rockets fired at the illuminated chopper always told us where the enemy was. The B-40, unfortunately, did not stop at the light but went on through the skin of the chopper and into the engine. It was interesting to note that helicopters, despite their ability to autorotate, simply do not glide when their engines stop. That's another reason why the visors cover the faces of the pilots—you can't see them scream as they fall a thousand feet inside heavy metal.

We didn't turn on the lights often.

Normally, we shot them out ourselves before takeoff.

That saved a lot of lives.

In retaliation, Colonel Black gave orders that we were to stay in the air all night. Helicopters don't have large gasoline tanks. Not all-night large. Not half-a-night large. Not more than two-or-three-hours large, as a matter of record. We sat down a lot and had tremendous poker games while the helicopter was being refueled.

Since the light didn't work as well as Colonel Black had hoped, he also installed a "people sniffer," which basically was a long black hose that hung next to the light. The hose was attached through a hole in the floor to a machine that would produce a loud sound when the hose passed through the gasses of methane and ammonia. As Colonel Black so vividly put it, "If they're shittin' and pissin', they're ours, men!"

Spec. 7 Thompson said, "It's a big black dick flying around in the Big Dick, controlled by a bunch of dicks and sniffing for dicks."

He was envious because he hadn't thought of it first.

Unfortunately, a lot of mammals shit and piss. The machine resulted in several herds of water buffalo, seven goats, and three monkeys going to that great methane farm in the sky. These results aroused great suspicion in the bugheads, and that's why one of them was watching me so closely as I finished throwing out the rest of the turds.

They gladly took me home, and I found the guys huddled around the monitoring screen, which was putting off a weird green light and adding a nice ambience to the bunker.

"How we gonna know if a sensor goes off?" asked Quiet Voice.

He had a point. How *were* we going to know? The manual had explained how to put out the turds—helicopters were not mentioned—and how to hook up the monitoring machine. It did not state how to monitor the Hughes Aircraft monitor machine number 637. It did not state what the machine did, just that it needed to be monitored.

So we monitored.

For three days.

Watching a green circle.

It was the most fun we'd had for months.

We all had bet what would happen when the enemy triggered a sensor. I said the machine would give us the exact coordinates, but not too many agreed with my theory. Most of them went with Thompson's idea that the green would change into a deeper shade of green. Because so much money was riding on the outcome, none of us dared leave. One would go make a sandwich or take a leak while the others watched the little green circle, commenting on the color green.

Colonel Black's idea had been refined thusly: We were to monitor the machine—which was what we were doing—and when it went off, we were to call the night-duty helicopter to our camp and put the 4.2 mortar, baseplates and all, along with ourselves—Shotgun, Quiet Voice, and me—into the helicopter. Along with us was to be the mobile rifle unit. Spec. 7 Thompson would relay information between us and Colonel Black, who would be standing by with the mobile mike mortar backup unit, a group of about twenty-one men ready to come to our rescue—all for dog turds.

Once airborne, we were to proceed to the activated sensor, sit down on the same sensor once it quit activating, set up the mortar, and fire on those who'd set off the sensors. If they returned fire, a likely circumstance in war, Colonel Black with his mobile force would quickly call back our helicopter, load his force onto it, and come to our rescue by annihilating the enemy, using the activated sensor as a guide.

It was pointed out to the colonel that one helicopter could not hold twenty-one men.

His reply was, "We'll do it in waves. Seven men per trip."

Quiet Voice raised his hand. "Have you ever heard of General Custer?"

The colonel gave a mad smile. "No."

The Night
of the Mobiles

It wasn't the different shades of green after all. On the fourth night, little white dots suddenly began dancing next to line 37 on the horizontal scale and line 8 on the vertical scale. These numbered vertical and horizontal lines matched the same vertical and horizontal lines on a map of our area.

Our maps called that place—the point at which line 37 horizontal and line 8 vertical intersected—the Plain of Reeds. But Hughes Aircraft worked only with verticals and horizontals, not maps and people.

Spec. 7 Thompson had retreated to his room and slammed the door. He was pouting about losing out on his "different shades of green" theory, but I had worse things to worry about.

Shotgun.

You could smell the cologne before you got to the mortar pit. He was wearing his best starched jungle fatigues; his boots were polished and his webbing was pressed. God! He looked strac. "Strac" is a word that has never been used by normal people. It's a word that means strategically perfect. See why normal people have never heard of it?

Anyway, I don't think Shotgun had ever looked better; well, maybe at his birthday party in Thailand, but he'd messed that up when he shot that Canadian through his side. The Thai police can really dirty a good uniform. But I digress.

"Let's roll, Shotgun," I shouted as I staggered through the cologne smell.

He grabbed his mortar in a lovely, moving hug.

"We're going to a party, baby."

It was good to see that they'd finished their quarrel. The last time they'd gotten into an argument, he'd fired all the mortar rounds trying to melt the barrel down. I had a feeling we'd need some mortar rounds tonight and was relieved to see they'd patched things up.

By the time we'd carried thirty rounds of mortar shells, baseplate, and mortar tube to the chopper pad, we could hear the incoming popping sound of the night-duty helicopter.

Shotgun was ecstatic.

I had a bad feeling.

"Where's the ten-man CIDG mobile rifle team for our protection?" asked Quiet Voice, who joined us late because more little dots had appeared on the green screen and he'd waited to plot their position on our field map. When too many dots appeared, he just gave up trying to mark them all and came out at the sound of the chopper to tell us about it.

Like I said, I had a real bad feeling.

Out of our Vietnamese counterparts' hootch came

five reluctants who owed their commander money they'd lost to him in a poker game. That they were not happy about going was clear because they kept shooting back at the hootch but doing little damage, since the hootch was covered in sandbags. This was good and bad.

Good because their fear of going proved they weren't Communists.

Bad because they were wasting valuable ammunition.

They refused to get into the chopper. One of them put a grenade under his arm and threatened to blow off his arm if we tried to make him go.

"Hell, he's going to die anyway," said Shotgun, walking over to the badly frightened individual, pulling the pin on the grenade under the man's arm, then hopping into the chopper. The man screamed, dropped the grenade, and followed Shotgun.

I have never seen a chopper loaded and airborne so fast.

The only reason I don't like flying with hysterical Vietnamese and Americans is that they shift their bodies so much, trying to keep away from the open doors, where bullets often enter. I like the bodies to stay still when I'm in the middle. I like the nice, thick bodies to stay perfectly still when I'm in the middle. I don't like bodies to sit perfectly still, staring in fear at Shotgun. Attention makes him nervous.

The chopper bugheads didn't set us down on 37 horizontal and 8 vertical because there are no lines drawn on real ground. This fact probably saved our lives.

We did sit down close, and our mobile rifle unit deployed quickly and professionally with their guns pointed towards the enemy:

Us.

Fortunately, the door gunner on the helicopter was able to drive them out into the Plain of Reeds and away from our mortar site. Shotgun didn't notice. He was too busy putting his "lovely" back together.

As we lay in the tall reeds that gave the plain its name, we heard the chopper lift off. For some reason its large jet-landing light was clicked on. It came on like a great star and illuminated the plains around us. We could see the muzzle of our mobile team trying to shoot out the light so we couldn't be seen. We joined them. But the helicopter flew on until it flew over the many little dots on the green screen. The explosion was deafening.

Lights went out.

Pilots went out.

Xing loi, Sweet Chariot.

"How we going to get back now?" Quiet Voice asked, a little concerned. "Who's going to pick up the colonel and his men?" he said anxiously. "How we going to get resupplied?" he screamed.

"Tell Shotgun not to fire! Maybe they won't realize we're here!" I yelled, but it was too late.

Chunkkkkk.

Chunkkkkk.

Karrrumph.

Karrrumph.

Crank.

Crank.

Crank, crank, crankcrankcrankcrankcrank.

The first two sounds are what a large mortar makes when its shells are leaving the earth.

The second two sounds are what a mortar shell sounds like when it's hitting the earth again.

The final sounds are a battalion of pissed-off AK-47s, the weapon of choice for crack North Vietnamese troops.

But that's not the bad news.

The Bad
News

Thompson. Spec. 7 Thompson. Remember? He's over his pout and is back at the monitor. We're in a world of shit, and he calls us on the horn.

"Bird Dog One, this is Bird Dog Three."

"Thompson, that call sign was five months ago! Turn five pages, find today's date, and use that call sign!" That's Colonel Black, monitoring the radio and straining at gnats while we're being eaten by *T. rex*.

"Roger. Wait one."

Crankcrankcrankcrankcrank I would put a period here but that would indicate the guns stopped shooting and they didn't.

Time is a great commodity when you don't have it.

"Irish Setter One. Irish Setter One, this is Irish Setter Three."

"Go ahead."

"Listen, how close are you to those sensors?"

"I have no idea."

"I sure hope you're not too close. Sensors are indicating another battalion is moving by them now real fast."

That's the bad news.

"Help me! My God, help me!" It was Shotgun.

Quiet Voice and I ran to the mortar. Actually, we crawled to the mortar, since our little band of CIDG troops had long since been absorbed or killed by the larger force *out there*, which, according to the latest sensor report, was getting larger.

"Pucker factor 9" is when a ten-penny nail cannot be driven up your asshole with a sledgehammer because your ass is too tight from fear.

We had a pucker factor 9.

"She's drowning, Captain, and I can't stop to save her! Don't let her die like this!"

Shotgun pointed at bubbling water around the baseplate. The Plain of Reeds was a water-soaked pasture with no solid land for the butt of a heavy lady. The tube was disappearing from the recoil of exiting shells Shotgun was feeding down it. As the tube disappeared the shells began walking back towards us because the angle was changing.

Follow the yellow exploding reed road, Wicked Witch of the North.

"What do we do now?" Quiet Voice.

"Get the fuck out of here!" My voice.

"Crankcrankcrankcrankcrank." Their voice.

"Irish Setter One?" Thompson's voice on radio.

"What!" Me again.

"Three dots just broke away from the large group and are moving north. No, wait! The other dots are swinging to follow them."

"Look, asshole, those three dots are us. Quit

telling them where we are!'' I wanted to shout the words but I had to whisper.

"Please, no cursing on the radio and use only the proper call sign, Irish Setter, when talking.'' Colonel Black.

You've seen the Plain of Reeds before: it's that area around your lake you always avoid because it's too gross to walk in; the one with the scum on it and frightful little bugs that scoot across and shit at the same time; that area close to the beach where crabs scuttle and things die in gray mud; every wet spot on a scout trip where the mud sticks in layers to your body and boots and weighs you down as you try to walk through it; that area that smells like someone farted into a pipe attached to your nose. Yes, you remember. The Plain of Reeds.

One special feature, one I definitely liked, was the tall, very tall, great-to-hide-in grass.

Quietly.

They're here, making those little sounds of hunting men everywhere, hoping to flush some game.

You are quail.

You are foxes.

You are little deer.

You swear you'll never hunt again.

Sweet Jesus!

There is a new species of a centipede-something slowly crawling up my rifle barrel. I don't dare move. I watch the insect crawl across my sights, onto my hand, up my sleeve. I can feel it on my skin. It crawls up my shoulder, hesitates, and starts down my back. It stops. It starts. It stops again. Each leg rotates on my nerves. It gets to my lower back. My head is dripping with sweat and I want to lay it on my rifle but dare not move. The insect is forgotten as footsteps squish by me. There are worse things than a crawling insect. I know that now.

The AN/PRC-25 radio crackles to life, scaring the hell out of everyone.

Radio carries well in the Plain of Reeds. We leave it quickly after booby-trapping it with a grenade. We leave slug trails in the gray slime. Large slug trails.

Crankcrankcrank . . . *boom!*

There goes the radio.

And one of their men.

No radio.

No ride.

We're in for the long crawl.

A Geography Lesson

Where's Idaho?'' It's the first thing Shotgun has said since he lost his mortar. Not that he said a lot when he had his mortar. We have been hiding for days on the Plain of Reeds, hoping Colonel Black will send us a chopper. He hasn't. We finished our last LRRP rations yesterday, eating the dehydrated food dry. Mine was sawdust, tasting vaguely of pepperoni pizza. What little water we have is used for drinking.

I crawl over to Shotgun to ask him not to stand up while asking questions. There are rules of conduct on the Plain of Reeds.

''Where's Idaho?'' he repeats with a puzzled frown.

I answer him quietly, so he has to squat to hear me.

''What do you mean, where's Idaho? It's in the United States, Shotgun.''

Shotgun grabs me by the lapels and jerks me to my feet—a definite breach of officer–enlisted man protocol—

however, the nervous tremors passing through Shotgun's body make me overlook this small incident.

"I know it's in the U.S., Captain, but is it close to Montana or New Orleans?"

"Montana, I think."

"Good! They haven't moved it yet."

"Why is that important just at this moment, Shotgun?" I was beginning to sound like Quiet Voice, who had rolled over in place and was peeing. You do that when you're hiding or on ambush. You don't stand. You just roll over and let it flow and hope you're uphill.

"It's where I'm going after I kill Colonel Black."

I breathe a sigh of relief. I'd been hoping Shotgun would blame the right person.

The problem is helping Shotgun get back to kill Black.

We need a radio in order to go.

Shot in the ass has no class.

Rhyming here.

On a roll.

I'm a poet.

Crankcrank . . .

Free-verse time.

"Give me your M-16 and I'll get us out of here," Shotgun says, smiling.

That doesn't give me confidence. I look at Quiet Voice. He shrugs his shoulders. Great help.

We've never seen Shotgun with an M-16. The army procedure is to certify competency before issuing a new weapon. I follow procedure:

"Who am I?"

Shotgun peers back at me through the grass. "You're my captain."

"And who's that?" I point to Quiet Voice.

"Gimme a hint."

"He asks a lot of questions."

"That's easy. Quiet Voice."

Shotgun turns and looks the other way through the grass.

"If you're my captain and he's Quiet Voice, then who's he?"

Crankcrankcrankcrank

We turn and fire together, shooting Who's He, a dirty little man in brown fatigues who looks frightened as he falls. We look frightened as we run. Touring the Plain of Reeds has that effect on people.

Shotgun mumbles something about a plan as we follow him through the Plain of Reeds, but I'm not sure if it's working or not. He never does tell us what his plan is, but here's what happens: We follow Shotgun into a very large river. We don't cross it. We float down it. Maybe we shouldn't call it "floating"; "swept away" seems to fit our screams better.

The army manual for Southeast Asian rivers states the following: "A rule of thumb when crossing jungle rivers is to assume the river is as deep as it is wide."

This river was a quarter mile across.

I couldn't touch bottom.

Nor swim.

It was preferable to where we'd been.

A Medical Breakthrough

There you are.

You're still at the river. We've crawled up onto the bank, thinking about blood flukes. Unless you're a doctor, they're unknown to you. Americans have many household pets—cats, dogs, parakeets—but the Orient is much more exotic. They have bird-eating spiders, small snakes called wait-a-minute snakes—one minute after they bite you, you're dead—and little creatures called blood flukes.

The symptoms aren't many. Having to take a shit every two seconds pretty well tells the story of blood flukes. If you can't take down your pants fast enough, that's blood flukes. If—and a lot of people don't get this far into blood flukes—clear liquid begins to come out your asshole and when you pinch your skin it stays up in a peak and people comment how you look like a prune, you've got about three days to live without medical attention.

"Captain, you look like a prune," said Shotgun.

Shotgun and Quiet Voice were huddled about twenty yards upwind from me on the banks of the river. Since the blood flukes and I were practicing our little number at the time, I really didn't pay any heed to Shotgun's comment. The Second Coming wouldn't have warranted a glance from me.

"Can you pinch your skin into a peak?" asked Quiet Voice, who sounded detached and scientifically curious.

I wiped my ass with my hand and dangled the dirty fingers in the river to clean them. The other hand gripped my stomach. I thought of Who's He, the little man we'd killed on the Plain of Reeds, and how lucky he was now as another wave of cramps washed through me.

Shotgun attempted to approach me, but the stench drove him away. "You've got blood flukes," he said. "It's just a matter of time until we all get them. Did you know they ride on your white corpuscles until they get into your liver? That's where they make their home. Ten years later, they finish off the liver. That's extremely rare, though. Most people are dead of dehydration by then."

That comforted me.

"Where are we?" I groaned as another wave of cramps rolled in.

Shotgun looked down the river. "Where we are doesn't matter; where we are going does."

I had the drizzling shits again. While there, I began to hear the Beatles singing "Let It Be." I was dying and it was good to know that rock and roll had been adopted in heaven. Surely the Beatles wouldn't be heard in hell.

Surely?

Quiet Voice stood up and looked around. "Where is the Beatle music coming from?" I was comforted to know that Quiet Voice heard the heavenly band, too. That meant he was going to join me wherever it was I was headed.

Shotgun ran to the edge of the river and began waving his arms wildly, which didn't make any sense to me. God knew where to find us.

Maybe.

"It's the Riverines! It's the goddamn navy! Hey, you motherfuckers, over here!" Shotgun's voice echoed across the river and bounced off two navy assault boats, one mounted with two very large speakers playing "Let It Be."

They didn't. The boats swung towards us firing their .50s. Shotgun and Quiet Voice held up their hands. My hands were busy with the blood flukes, and a prayer came from my lips.

"Let them be good shots and put me out of this misery."

Amen.

It's Not Kansas

"*Who are you?*" The loudspeakers onboard the PT boat blasted the shore where Shotgun and Quiet Voice stood and I shitted—or is it "shat"?

"We're Americans," shouted Shotgun, "trying to get to Idaho."

Why he added that, I don't know. Shotgun wasn't crazy, but the guys on the boats were. They fired another burst of .50s above our heads. Some tree limbs seven inches thick fell around me. I grabbed the leaves. They were better than my fingers. Smoother, too.

"No, you're not! Americans don't look like you."

"Okay, then, we're North Vietnamese who want to *chieu hoi*." That's "give up," in Vietnamese.

Another burst of .50s. More leaves. I'm grateful.

"No, you're not! North Vietnamese don't look like you."

"How about human beings?" suggested Quiet Voice.

Another burst of .50s.

"Maybe." Contact. "What smells so bad?"

"The captain. He's sick."

The guy behind the .50s shouted, "No shit, Sherlock. All officers are."

Shotgun looked at me.

"He's got a little left," he shouted. "Could we catch a ride home?"

"Burn your clothes first."

"We're not wearing any. They rotted off days ago."

"Then, what's . . . ?"

"Caked mud."

"We'll throw you a rope and drag you behind the boat until you come clean. Otherwise, no deal."

"What about the captain?" Quiet Voice wasn't going to leave me after all.

"Shoot him."

"Thank you," I managed to say before doubling over again.

Shotgun held on to me while the river washed away our sins. I lay on my back in the wake of the boat, safe, while the arm of Shotgun held me above water. I had to tap the arm occasionally when it tightened around my neck, but that happened only when Shotgun began raving about the colonel.

Later, when we lay drying on the deck, we asked them why they played such beautiful music.

Their captain wanted them to sail up and down the river playing Beatle music night and day. The sound of the music was to tip off the enemy the two boats were coming and give the NVA time to set up an ambush. When the NVA began firing, the two boats would remain on station—how could they leave?—and call in a mobile naval air strike on the ambush.

But things had not worked out as planned.

We nodded our heads knowingly.

"It's at night that we have our problems," one zit-faced navy kid was explaining as he dug deeper into his nose for an elusive something. "The villagers don't like being waked up at three in the morning by the Beatles. They get angry after two or three nights running. That's when the trouble starts. They're so crazy from lack of sleep, they shoot at us. We report the shots, our captain says it's an enemy ambush, and the village is destroyed."

The navy kid found what he'd been looking for and held it up admiringly for all to see. Then he frowned, saying, "We're killing everyone along the river but the captain doesn't want us to stop because our kill ratio is the highest in the delta."

Shotgun became agitated. Actually, he started "agitating" when the kid mentioned a "mobile" air strike. I made a mental note not to use that term around Shotgun anymore.

"Where did your captain graduate from?" asked Quiet Voice as I hung my ass over the gunwale, stoned out of my mind on the ten ounces of opium-rich paregoric given to me by the boat's medic. It didn't make me quit shitting, but I no longer cared, which was just as good.

"Princeton."

My ass clamped shut. I had a bad feeling.

"Captain?" asked Quiet Voice. "Why are we going upriver towards the Plain of Reeds?"

Shotgun and Quiet Voice joined me at the gunwale.

Orders

O rders" is an antonym for "common sense."

There was a battalion of NVA waiting for the navy upriver, and the safety of our camp was downriver.

Using common sense, Shotgun was explaining the situation to the commander of the boats, a young jg named Sergio Baeza from Santa Fe. He was a long way from the Sangre de Cristo Mountains. Every time Shotgun explained why we needed to go downriver, the young jg replied that his orders were to find the enemy.

Shotgun nodded in agreement. "The enemy, sir, is downriver." And he leaned over and whispered something in the officer's ear.

"But that's your commanding officer!" said the young man, in complete shock.

Shotgun nodded again. He was making headway.

"You're crazy, Sergeant!" said the stupid young jg.

Quiet Voice and I ducked behind a bulkhead.

The diplomacy of a magazine of bullets fired against the steel of the ship was a dramatic display of tact by Shotgun. Such restraint was not lost on the young officer.

The boat turned around. I tried to smooth things over with the rest of the guys.

"The navy can adapt: from sails to steam, steam to diesel, upriver to downriver."

While Quiet Voice kept them covered, I lay on the deck and sang along with the music.

> *"And in my hour of darkness,*
> *She is standing right in front of me*
> *Speaking words of wisdom,*
> *'Let it be.'"*

A white Asian egret flew over the deck. I could not remember having seen a bird in the delta before. It was so beautiful, with its large white wings outstretched and its golden legs straight out behind. It was nice to know there were a few living things left.

Another swig on the old paregoric and the egret flew back in the other direction. It was red now, with a yellow tail.

"B-40 rocket!" I heard someone say.

"Incoming!" I heard Shotgun say.

These were not familiar names for the egret. I tried to tell them they were mistaken in identifying the egret as such, but either I slurred the words or they just ignored me. I lay on the deck, feeling the hot shell casing from the .50s bounce off my skin. It was different. Another swig on the old paregoric.

The jg and Shotgun were friends now. The boat

swung towards the ambush and the radio crackled alive.

The Beatles played on.

The jets roared in from the South.

The little men fired from the North.

Orange napalm flowed west to east, following the banks of the river.

I lay in the crossroads, shitting my guts out.

Home

Spec. 7 Thompson wouldn't let us in.

"Come on, Thompson, open the gate," I said, using my best command voice. It didn't work.

I could see Thompson peeking over the burnt jeep by the main gate.

"You couldn't be alive," he said. "Colonel Black reported you missing in action two weeks after we lost radio contact with you. Besides, when did you join the navy? What's wrong with the army?"

Since it was now dark, how Thompson could tell we were dressed in navy clothes was a mystery. Maybe the light from a new night-duty helicopter flying directly over our heads helped him identify our clothes. The fact we had our hands on our heads, fingers laced together, hoping no idiot would shoot us, may have helped, also.

Even Pecker, our camp dog, didn't recognize us. He never barked at Americans, just foreigners. He sat on his haunches next to Thompson and growled. Thompson patted him on the head for encouragement. Pecker was a real big dog. We could have taken Thompson, but not Thompson and Pecker.

Sounds like a British law firm, doesn't it?

"What's our new call sign?" Thompson shouted from behind the gate.

"It's some kind of dog. Let's see. . . . We were on Irish Setter when we lost the radio; so, working our way up the alphabet, we're probably in the *l*'s by now. How about Labrador?"

There was a moment of stunned silence behind the fence. We could hear pages being flipped. "Lucky guess," Thompson shouted. "But you left off 'Retriever.'"

Shotgun tapped me on the shoulder with his elbow. "Why did the colonel say we missed the action? He's the one who missed the action." His lips got thin.

Quiet Voice spoke softly from beside Shotgun. "What was that the navy guys called us—some kind of animal?"

Shotgun glanced at Quiet Voice. "It was some kind of bird—egret or something."

"Albatross," I muttered.

"Whatever. Navy guys are so superstitious. After the B-40s, they were happy to bring us back."

"Who pitched in the 1935 World Series?" Thompson was warming up to his new role as guardian of the camp.

I was growing disgusted. "Damn it, Thompson. I grew up in West Texas. There weren't enough people in a three-hundred-mile radius to play cards with, much less baseball. Why in the hell would I know who won the 1935 World Series?"

"That proves you're not an American!" Thompson shouted, and fired a burst over our heads, driving us to our stomachs.

Quiet Voice was tugging at my sleeve.

"Not now, Quiet Voice."

"Sir, what time is it?"

"What time is—Quiet Voice, why is that so important right now. Anyway, I don't have a watch."

"What time is it, Thompson?" shouted Quiet Voice.

"Ten P.M. Why?"

"Isn't that the time we usually get shelled?"

Karrumph.

Karrumph.

We heard Thompson scream, "Shit," then saw him sprinting for the middle triangle, Pecker on his heels. But he forgot to open the gates.

It didn't matter.

The first two rounds blew them open.

It was good to be home.

Mail Call

Our letters were already opened.

We glanced at Thompson, who gave a sheepish shrug. "Hey, if you had truly been dead I'd have forwarded these to your next of kin—no problem."

I tilted an empty care package from home and shook it. One lonely chocolate chip with a few weeks' mold fell like an anvil on the table. We all stood there, silently looking at the chip.

"C'mon guys! You don't think I'd be cold enough to eat your food packages from home?" Thompson said indignantly. We looked from the chip to Thompson and back to the chip again.

Little beads of sweat broke out on the Spec. 7's forehead.

"Look, tell you what I'm going to do," he said, disappearing into his bed cubicle. Shotgun snapped up his grenade launcher, his new weapon of choice, at the sudden movement.

"Whoa, big fellow," Thompson said, popping back out. "Look what I have."

In his arms Thompson carried boxes of letters and sex magazines. He dumped them on the table, mixing them with ours.

"The mail chopper that brought out the mail came under heavy fire just as it was landing, so it just pitched off several duffel bags full of mail. Beats the shit out of me who most of this stuff belongs to, but, man, is it good reading!"

Shotgun put the grenade launcher over his shoulder and grabbed a handful of letters.

"That's it," Thompson encouraged us all. "Just pretend like they've all been written to you."

We grabbed as many as we could after Shotgun got his, and we each went off to our little cubicles to lie on our bunks and read about the world. Spec. 7 Thompson slumped in a chair, exhausted from his near-death experience.

The first letter I read was to Quiet Voice. It was from his mother:

Dear soldier,

Guess what we got waiting for you at home—a puppy! You know how your Aunt Madge always pours hot water on bitches in heat? Well, she did it on a pregnant one and she dropped them puppies on Madge's front lawn in about two seconds flat. We managed to save one of them. Madge scalded the other four.

I hope your taking a bath regularly. We

read about some of those tropical diseases and worry about them getting loose over here. I know it's hard to remember these things but hang up your towels after bathing. That's where diseases of the private parts come from.

Janice says she misses you. Did I tell you she married Harry Shulberg, the shop foreman? He says you can have your old job back but not your old girlfriend. Ha. Ha.

The President says the war is going good. Is it?

Love you,
Mom

I could hear Quiet Voice laughing down the hall. It was good to see morale picking back up after the Plain of Reeds. I glanced at two more letters: one was to someone named Armstrong; it was from his wife, who had joined a local church and had accepted Christ into her heart. Her church-sponsored support group had urged her to write this letter asking for a divorce. It was the Christian thing to do, since she could no longer live with a killer. It was signed with her name and a peace symbol. The other letter was to a guy named Eisenhart. It was from a car dealership. They were threatening to "repo" his car because he'd missed the monthly car payments.

It was funny as hell, their threatening to have him arrested and tried in a Maryland court. No wonder Eisenhart, whoever he was, wasn't making the monthly payments. He was hoping the dealership would come get him and take him home. It beat shooting yourself in the foot.

Quiet Voice appeared at the door, chuckling. "You

want to trade, Captain?'' I traded him an Armstrong and an Eisenhart for three letters, the bottom one of which was to Shotgun.

The first thing to fall out of the letter was a monthly receipt. I glanced at the amount. It was over half of Shotgun's monthly salary. The receipt was crudely made and had dirt on one corner. It was signed by a priest, Father Rodrigo Carreras, from la Escuela de la Acequia Madre para los Niños sin Padres.

Next was a letter from Father Carreras to Shotgun:

Dear Señor,

I regret to inform you that the school you and your men built here in Bolivia was destroyed last night by either the guerrillas or government forces. Neither claims responsibility. Unfortunately, most of the children died in the attack. I found your letter to Fr. Enrico Calderon in the rubble the next morning and I am sending it back with a request for more money. We will rebuild the school and, with help like yours, once again educate the new children who will soon arrive.

Con Cristo,
Fr. Carreras

P.S. I am puzzled by your hatred of education. Be at peace, my son.

Was Shotgun ever at peace? He'd been in Bolivia in 1967 to train Bolivian *lanceros* in the fine art of guerilla hunting. They'd found Che Guevara's band with the help of the local Indians, who were quite incensed that someone with a northern urban accent would try to foment revolution in South America. He had done the job well. His only comment on the operation was, "Che Guevara was set up by Castro. I just did his dirty work for him."

"Why would Castro want to set up Che Guevara?" I asked, not wanting to show my ignorance.

"Lots of reasons. Rewrite history, for one. Guevara was the leader of the Cuban Revolution in fifty-six."

"I thought it was Fidel Castro."

"Fidel couldn't fight his way out of a cleared rain forest. Che Guevara was the leader and the men followed him. You know why?"

"Why?"

"He kept them alive. Fidel was a doctor's son. I never trusted doctor's sons. What did your father do?" he asked.

"He was a rancher," I said, hoping ranchers' sons didn't appear on his shit list.

I glanced at the next letter. It had been mailed six months before. The army was having a hard time finding Shotgun. Didn't we all? I glanced inside the envelope at the yellowing, brittle sheet of paper. Taking it out and unfolding it, I was surprised to see it was from Shotgun. I had never seen him write. I read the military-style letter:

TO: Father Enrico Calderon
SUBJECT: Education of Children
REFERENCE: WW II, Korea, Vietnam

When I was a young private in WW II, I was impressed with the fine craftsmanship of Krupp Steel. Their weapons were far superior to ours. The V-rockets were far superior to any weapons we had; their tanks had angled steel to deflect antitank weapons; their rifles had longer ranges and held more bullets. I was impressed with the minds behind the weapons.

Then we found those camps with human beings branded like cattle, ovens still warm from cooking little children, and boxes filled with gold fillings. I began to wonder, standing in the camps, how educated people could do this.

Germany had the best educational system of its time in Europe. It was educated engineers who built the gas chambers; educated chemists who made the gas; educated doctors who sewed eyeballs on backs to see if the eyeballs would still work; and, above all, educated teachers who convinced minds it was permissible and honorable to do these things for patriotism.

And you ask me what kind of education I want for the orphans? Are you fucking crazy or what?

I want you to teach them to be human beings first. Don't teach them history. They'll only repeat it. Take my money and spoil them. Get them candy, buy them books they want to read, not those mandated by the state or church, and let them go swimming and take them to play in the snows of the Andes. Maybe this bunch will make it.

End of letter.

Well, the kids hadn't made it, and I debated whether or not to show the letter to Shotgun. Still, he needed to know. I folded up the letter and stuffed it, with the other items, back into the envelope. I walked down the hall, out the door, and over to the mortar pit. Shotgun was sitting beside the hole where his mortar used to be. I handed him the letter.

"Did you read it?" he asked as he read the contents.

"No," I lied.

Shotgun looked at me for a long time. "It's just as well," he said as he took a chunk of C-4 explosive putty and struck a match to it. It flared instantly. He held the letter and its contents over the flame until it burned his fingers. He pushed the ashes slowly into the empty mortar hole.

"That letter got more of a burial than those kids did, Captain."

"What are you going to do now, Shotgun?"

"Send them two-thirds of my paycheck," he said, and walked away. Over his shoulder, he said, "One of the bunches will make it. Somebody's got to pull us a little farther out of the mud."

Shotgun the humanitarian?

It's a strange damn world.

Off to See
the Colonel

I had hoped the letters would take Shotgun's mind off his promise to kill Colonel Black. Not that he would, of course. That's crazy. In the Plain of Reeds a lot of things might have been said that weren't really meant. We'd even gone along with Shotgun's fantasy by suggesting ways to kill the colonel, but that was just to pass the time while we hid in the grass.

A week went by and life was returning to abnormal. I had ordered Spec. 7 Thompson not to report us found for a few days so Shotgun could get over the loss of his mortar. Everyone else knew not to mention Colonel Black's name.

So there we were, crouched in a bunker, listening to the steel rain, when a voice in the darkness said, "Aren't those explosions too loud to be Vietnamese mortars?"

And, like a fool, I laughed and answered, "Yeah,

it's probably Colonel Black welcoming us home.'' Immediately, I regretted what I had said, but it was too late. Shotgun gave a graveyard moan and sprinted from the bunker.

To understand this next part, you'll have to go out to your garage and start your lawnmower. Actually, you should go steal a lawnmower because Shotgun stole a Honda motorbike from one of our counterparts to go kill the colonel.

That's it—pull the cord, flip the switch, turn the handle, squeeze the trigger.

Putputputput. That's what it sounds like, right? Now, drive it back inside the garage. Shut the door.

Putputputputput

That's what it sounded like when Shotgun drove the Honda into the Bunker and asked us if we wanted to go with him. You can turn off the lawnmower, please.

Thanks. Off he drove, CAR-15 slung over his back, M-79 grenade launcher across the handlebars, and two Randall knives strapped to his side. I suppose he faded off down the road, but since the shelling continued, we didn't give him a proper sendoff.

We should have.

It was Colonel Black shelling us.

He was trying out his latest idea, a floating mortar pit, on the Vam Co Tay River. At the moment, he and his men were stuck on a sandbar and were trying to use the recoil from the mortar to shake loose.

What's a Randall knife? A little guy in Florida made them in a special way so they could cut through bone or steel cable without breaking or losing their edge. He was our sword maker—our metal wizard. By the way his name was—ready for this?—Randall. Back to the story:

The next part is a little fuzzy. It loses something in

the translation. Had I been there, it would have been better, but since I got it secondhand, be patient.

Apparently, Shotgun drove right past the men on the sandbar in his mad dash on the Honda to Moc Hoa. That flows, doesn't it? I think I'll say it again. "A mad dash on the Honda to Moc Hoa."

When he got to Moc Hoa and found out where the colonel was, Shotgun borrowed a sampan and began the trip back up the Vam Co Tay River.

In the meantime Colonel Black and his men were still shelling us because they were still stuck on the sandbar. But things were getting better, for every shell fired was less weight on the boat. They were making progress. But so was the tide.

Low tide.

Just as they broke free they heard the sampan coming up the river behind them like the sound of a thousand angry bees. When Colonel Black turned and saw Shotgun, who, in the colonel's mind, was still missing in action and presumed dead, he panicked. He might have panicked because Shotgun was firing his M-79 grenade launcher at him, but most agree it was because he thought that what he was seeing was Shotgun's ghost.

Screaming in fear, he shifted the mortar and began trying to shell Shotgun. The recoil drove him back up onto the sandbar. And since the tide was lower, the boat struck an old mine, which had probably been there since the French colonial days. It would have taken a hard hit with a sledgehammer to get the rusty old thing to blow up.

Or the recoil from a floating mortar pit, which was an impossibility until Colonel Black's time.

The spring-loaded mine bounded out of the mud right under the colonel and the mortar, turning everything into a frothy mist.

There was a moment of silence.

Then loud cheering from the colonel's men, who had jumped from the floating mortar pit the minute they saw Shotgun.

The B team tried to console Shotgun by putting him in for a Silver Star for trying to save the colonel's life by driving a sampan at great disregard for his own life into a known underwater minefield and firing an M-79 grenade launcher to try and alert the floating mortar patrol of the floating danger.

It was to no avail. Shotgun had had his second loss, and nothing could cheer him anymore—nothing except a new colonel who was as mad as Colonel Black.

We decided to buy him a pet to try and rescue him from his deep depression.

Miss Ass Breath turned out to be a mistake.

Love Is a Many-splintered Thing

Shotgun was talking to someone in the mortar pit. He was murmuring terms of endearment, which made us all think of home. That was bad for morale. I went out to stop it. Actually, I went out to satisfy my curiosity. I didn't think he would forget Colonel Black or the loss of his beloved mortar so soon.

He was talking to the monkey we'd given him.

Don't worry about Shotgun. It was a *female* monkey. The thing is, he was handing her a piece of Doublemint gum, still wrapped. Since she was a primate, she had no trouble unwrapping the gum, popping it into her mouth, and chewing it.

Since she was a lower primate, she did have trouble figuring out what to do with the gum after she'd chewed it for a while. A monkey in a gum cocoon is not a pretty sight, but since Shotgun's mouth was in a tight pattern, I knew I should laugh, too. So I did.

"Captain, I want you to meet Miss Ass Breath." Shotgun said this as though he was announcing a debutante at a ball. I dropped the smile and shook her gum-sticky paw. She panicked when her paw stuck to my hand, and she jerked it free, the effort making her smack her gum-covered face with the gum-sticky paw.

She began to stretch the gum as she tried to pull her stuck paw from her face. With her free hand, she tried to swipe the gum strands between her face and her captured paw. Then, like a Navajo rug weaver, she took the gum back and forth between her hands, creating a web of gum.

I watched this until she couldn't move.

"Why do you call her Ass Breath, Shotgun?" I said, watching the struggling cocoon.

He pointed at her jaws. "See those bags beneath her cheeks? When I feed her food, she stores it there. Sometimes for days. Here, smell."

Shotgun grabbed the immobilized animal and held her up in front of my face. She was screaming from somewhere deep inside the gum but I could still smell her breath.

Her breath smelled like mint-flavored puke.

Garbage behind the hotel after three days.

Mouthwash with a red tide.

"Watch her for me, Captain. For tonight? It's not much to ask, and she'll be safer in your room."

I stared at Shotgun holding the maddened, screaming, breathing animal towards me. Was it a trick? Why me?

Sure, it's easy for you to say. "Take her into your room. Clean her up." But consider:

What if Shotgun liked her that way? With gum? See my point?

"How long do I need to keep her, Shotgun?"

"Just until the attack is over."

I looked around the perimeter. The day was hot, muggy, and almost over. Every day ended like that. I watched the sun touch a rice paddy. He placed the gummed monkey in my arms. She stuck to me like—well, like a gummed monkey. Her breath . . . her breath . . . her breath . . . Wait a minute, I'm searching for words. . . . Her breath smelled worse than the Plain of Reeds. My eyes began to water. Shotgun put his island-size hand on my shoulder and gave it a shake.

"Hey, Captain. Don't worry about me. I'll be all right out here during the attack."

I tried to focus on Shotgun. "What attack?"

"The one tonight."

Monkey See, Monkey Panic

And Shotgun was right. There was an attack. Some people have a twinge in the knee when the weather is going to change; others, their back acts up if it's going to snow. With Shotgun, his trigger finger cramped, old powder burns flared on his cheek, shrapnel fell out of his ears. He knew.

I had placed Miss Ass Breath in my hootch. She had crawled to one of my rifles—it was hanging on a crude wall rack—and rocked herself to sleep swinging on the sling. I tied a little rope to her neck, leaving enough room for her to crawl down off her perch and get a sip of water or some fresh cucumbers from bowls on the floor. I had to estimate the length of the rope. The thought of Miss Breath hanging herself in my room sent shudders through me.

I was sleeping on the floor when Spec. 7 Thompson called in the air strike. He had saved a few of the dog turds and placed them in the wire around the camp. We thought he just watched the monitor because of the green. Thompson was like that.

He told us later that when he saw that the sappers were in the wire, he wanted to get the bombs as close as possible to stun them.

"When they're stunned, it's like shooting fish in a rain barrel," he explained loudly to us, since we didn't hear as well then as we had before the sniper attack and the B-52s. Heavy metal does that to the ears.

Sappers are the elite athletes of the other team. They're trained to infiltrate camps like ours for no other reason than to blow things up—like us, for instance. They've been known to take five days to crawl four hundred feet. The North Vietnamese sappers glued grass to their backs and then watered it to blend in with the environment around the wire. Real back-to-nature guys. They carried little bags of grenades, which weren't that difficult to work, and large satchel charges, which were that hard to work. And B-40 rockets.

To do this work requires nerves of steel. Since they were human beings, they glued little vials of pure opium to their necks and put syringes into their veins. They knew their nerves were like all soldiers' nerves, not made of steel but of flesh. Dying hurt.

Of course, stoned out of their minds, they could create havoc—for themselves as well as others. That was why I was sleeping on the floor when the first B-52 bomb exploded ten yards from our camp.

Ten yards.

Thirty feet.

Three hundred and sixty inches.

I woke up. And realized I was blind. But not deaf. I knew the concussion was buckling my walls because I could feel the dust as it fell on my flak jacket and clothes. I could hear (sense?) my tin lampshade on the single overhead light slam in a swinging arc back and forth against the ceiling. But I was still blind.

My first thought, when my senses returned, was that I had climbed back up onto my bunk in my sleep and a B-40 rocket had decided to sleep with me. Sappers had a nasty habit of firing their rockets three feet off the ground so sleeping soldiers in three-foot-off-the-ground bunks could sleep permanently.

My next thought, as long fingernails began to scratch me, was that Shotgun had let me down and allowed the sappers to jump me on the floor. Fortunately, I could feel my weapon beside me and I swung it wildly in front of myself, spraying the cement room.

After the bullets quit bouncing around, I realized that I was bleeding and I could smell urine all over my neck. But I was still blind. There was only one thing to do: run.

In the darkness and bombed silence I felt for the door. The rush of air when the door opened was immediately replaced by rough hands grabbing me by the lapels.

"Cheating on me! You were cheating on me!" And Shotgun ripped Ass Breath from my face. At that moment I preferred the B-52s.

"Why was she sitting on your face?" said Shotgun, glaring at me with maniacal eyes. Actually, those were his normal eyes.

"Shotgun, she was trying to protect an American soldier." The eyes blinked. I had him on patriotism.

"Just like her. Sorry I roughed you up, sir. We got sappers in the wire. C'mon." We left Ass Breath and ran towards the berm.

They weren't in the wire.

They were through it.

But I didn't care. My life was mine again. It was mine again if I could keep those five little men now in our machine-gun bunker from turning it around and shooting us.

"They're in the machine-gun bunker!" Thompson always had to state the obvious. The bullets raked our position, which was flat and down. It's amazing how large a helmet gets in combat. I was doing chin-ups inside my helmet.

A furry primate having a nervous breakdown rushed over us and to the left of the pit. Since stoned sappers shoot at anything that moves, they swung towards Ass Breath, giving us time to kill them all. Shotgun kept shooting long after they were dead. He was the jealous type.

"That's for shooting at my pet!" he would shout, and fire a burst.

"That's for scaring her away!" Another burst. But though the bodies flopped, they didn't answer.

"Pets don't run away, Shotgun," I said, trying to soothe him. "She'll be back in the morning." It seemed to work. After an hour, he relaxed.

We lay there all night. Quietly.

"Why are we being so quiet if they're all dead?" asked Quiet Voice.

"Because," answered Thompson, "I counted six on the monitor."

That's why we lay there all night. Where were six? We didn't sleep well. The five bodies lay under the stars, close to four bodies who could still see them. Behind us, the camp slept.

We must have dozed. And we would have kept right on dozing if it hadn't been for Shotgun's screams of anguish. We awoke to the bright sun of midmorning.

"The bitch left me! Cleared out! She's nowhere around!"

And Miss Ass Breath was gone. We followed her tracks as they went towards the wire and disappeared. As we stood on top of the berm, trying to look into the new bomb craters to see if maybe she was hiding there, a little girl with grass glued to her back stood up.

"*Chieu hoi,*" she said holding her hands up. "*Chieu hoi.*"

Spec. 7 Thompson smiled. "Told you there were six."

Later, through an interpreter, she said her father had asked her to wait until he died, then surrender to the Americans. He had told her that his particular line of work had its drawbacks, one of which was crawling for two days through razor wire with a daughter clinging to the legs; the other was dying. Sappers couldn't buy life insurance to help out the family, so they just left them with us.

"Which one is your father?" asked Quiet Voice, pointing at the five still bodies.

She shrugged her shoulders. It was hard to tell. Shotgun's anger can confuse a little girl.

Shotgun said the girl was an omen. "Miss Ass Breath leaves and a little girl is sent." He took her by the hand and led her through the wire, careful to lift her over the sharp razor coils. We stood on the berm and watched him take her over to the water tank and begin cleaning the glued-on grass off her back.

"Call B team. Tell them to come get my daughter out of here," said Shotgun.

"She's not your dau—" Thompson grunted as I hit him in the ribs with my rifle butt.

"Do it," I ordered.

They sent out a chopper and the little girl climbed on board. She waved good-bye to Shotgun but he didn't notice. He was pouring lime on the five dead men, one of whom was her father. Shotgun was all heart.

Christmas Toys

They shipped the colonel home in a black box. Actually, they shipped what wasn't the colonel home in a black box. They do that often in a war. If there isn't anything left of the human being, they send a black box home nailed shut. It gives the hometown something to look at.

For every black box that goes home, another box appears at the A camp, whose appearance is quite capable of causing more black boxes to be sent home.

That's why we left the large gray box sitting on our chopper pad.

We let it sit there because Shotgun wouldn't let us go get it. "Whenever a gray box arrives, we have a new mission, which causes more black boxes to be sent home, which causes more gray boxes to be sent to us, which causes..." I was beginning to have an uneasy feeling.

Black boxes also bring replacements. The B team replaced Colonel Black with Col. Robert Basshore, an unusually large man from El Centro, California, who thought everything was a real sumbich.

"Men, this upcoming mission is a real sumbich. I haven't got all the details yet, but when I come back, I'll square this mission away."

He arrived at camp one day bringing two mission "specialists" to assist us in the upcoming sumbich. Naturally, the specialists had to have an officer, who would stay in camp to monitor his specialists.

The specialist monitor: 2d Lt. Jonathan Powell.

Sad-eyed, lost, beagle-face Powell. His hands seemed too delicate for the frayed cuffs on the uniform that cloaked him like an ill-fitted academic robe.

The new men scared Shotgun, which scared us.

"They don't send replacements unless they need to replace someone, and we're still here."

I looked around. He was right. We were still there—physically. Quiet Voice, Shotgun, Spec. 7 Thompson, and I. We shook their hands as if they were a bad case of blood flukes. Rookies have a way of injuring key players or replacing them.

After the colonel left, we turned our attention to the "FNGs" (Fucking new guys).

Top Sergeant Whitson was a black E-7 from Harlem. He was to be our mission intelligence chief, leading us in and out of the target area. He spoke the language of our target area natives. His cold, dark eyes reminded me of Shotgun. He was too tall and extremely thin and nervous, like a thoroughbred. He looked like a tall piece of black spaghetti, so we gave him a tag—Spaghetti. He loved to walk around and quote African proverbs as a solution to any problem. He had neat answers to Quiet Voice's questions, so he fit right in.

Quiet Voice would ask, "Why won't you tell us where we're going?"

And he would answer, "The truth is like gold; keep it locked up and you will find it exactly as you first put it away."

"Are there going to be a lot of firefights?" Quiet Voice again.

The answer: "The opportunity that God sends does not wake up him who is asleep."

Both of those quotes, he informed us, were from Senegal, which probably explains that country's position of importance in the world.

Buck Sgt. Randolph Subervich was from the coal mines of Pennsylvania. He was formerly a good half-back for Penn State, but a knee injury had cost him his scholarship. It was a tough injury, since it wasn't bad enough to keep him out of the war. He had been sent to show us how to use the items in the gray box still sitting on the chopper pad. There was just one problem. Actually, there were two. Shotgun wouldn't allow anyone, including the FNGs, to touch the box, and Subervich had only seen the items in the box. He hadn't been trained to use them.

"My security clearance didn't come in time for them to train me before my orders said I had to be here. So they just sent me."

"What did they send us?" asked Quiet Voice.

"Beats me," said Subervich. "That's classified."

"But we've got to use those things," I said.

"I'll figure out how to use them," said Thompson.

A black hand touched his chest. "Let me see your clearance."

The real puzzle was 2d Lt. Jonathan Powell. He had been sent to help us, but I'm not sure what he helped us with. He was one of those faces from American college classes, the kind that absorb everything but learn nothing.

He was thirty-two, a professor of philosophy from one of those little colleges in California. One night around the mashed potatoes, he tried to explain to all of us the nihilistic position of the existentialist and how that dovetailed in his mind with the law of entropy.

We all stared at him. Everybody except Shotgun.

He stared at his mashed potatoes.

"The universe is ruled by chaos and chance, not order! That's what entropy proves." Lieutenant Powell was excited.

"Everybody pick up your plate of potatoes," said Shotgun.

We did.

"Throw the plates in the air."

We did.

They all came down on the potato side.

Shotgun looked at Lieutenant Powell. "Bullshit."

But don't think Shotgun didn't like Second Lieutenant Powell. He felt sorry for all lieutenants. He gave me a card when I made captain. He'd made it himself on our psychological-warfare printer, which we usually reserved for making leaflets to drop on villages, telling them we were coming. The card's message was a meaningful one:

> Officers are like alligators. When they are lieutenants, you feel sorry for them and take care of them. When they reach captain, you keep them at arm's length. When they reach major, you hunt them, and when they are colonels, you kill them for trophies. Congratulations on your promotion, Captain.
>
> Shotgun—

He was always helpful like that. So that's why I know he liked Second Lieutenant Powell. Even if he didn't care much for Powell's philosophy.

We didn't see much of Powell. He stayed in his bunker and nursed a fifth of Everclear a day. His wife had found work in a lesbian bar in Los Angeles—just until he got back. He thought it was bad for her. But her letters seemed relaxed.

We read every one of them. They were great. She was one hell of a descriptive writer and enjoyed her work at the bar, which was servicing the customers. I wanted to visit that bar when I got back.

The gray box.

The gray box was still on the chopper pad. One night, Shotgun actually fell asleep. He hadn't slept well since the mortar problem, but time heals all wounds—time and stitches.

Finally Quiet Voice said, "I wonder what's in the box?"

We thought that over for hours, hoping Shotgun would wake up, but he slept on. And the monsoon was starting, too. He was sleeping through even that.

Monsoon?

Get into your shower. Turn it on. Turn it off. Turn it on. Turn it off. Do that night and day for about three months and you will understand monsoon.

Leaving the box in the rain was a mistake. I admit that. But how was I to know that labels wash off?

When we finally got the big gray box open, we looked inside and saw hundreds of little gray boxes. The first gray box I opened had a smaller gray box inside of it.

Shotgun was awake by then, but it was too late.

There was a small white ring sticking out of the

little gray box. I handed it to Lieutenant Powell, who handed it to Subervich, the gray-box specialist.

"Go outside and pull it," said Powell. "You're the only one with the necessary clearance to use it."

We all stared at Subervich, who was looking at the box. He walked a safe distance away from us and pulled the ring. It was attached to some thread. He kept pulling the ring and more thread came out. Leaving the box on the ground, he began walking back towards us, the ring hooked over his finger. More thread followed him.

We backed up.

He followed.

So did even more thread.

"It's a gray box with black thread in it!" he hollered, to keep us from backing over the berm. We all stopped.

I examined the thread and the box. Spec. 7 Thompson pulled and broke the string. The box hummed.

We jumped behind the berm.

And watched it.

It began to rain.

The box hummed in the rain.

We stayed behind the berm.

Disgusted, Lieutenant Powell picked up the box and cursed God.

Nothing happened.

Spec. 7 Thompson took the box inside, took it apart, and explained its meaning to us as we dried off.

"This is a camping device. You place the box by your ear, take the string and run it around your perimeter, couple a trees, a few bushes, and hook it back on the side of the black box. An animal or little men in black pj's break the string, it hums in your ear, you wake up, shoot something, and go back to sleep. We'll call it . . . "—he searched for a name—" . . . the humm box."

There were at least a thousand humm boxes in that large crate. But there were other things, too.

Clorox bottles. Lots of them.

Large brown coffee cans with the word "Schick" marked on them. We thought they were shaving kits until Quiet Voice asked, "What's that?"

"That" turned out to be a trigger on the side of the can.

"Do shaving kits have triggers?"

I couldn't answer Quiet Voice, so I had the coffee cans stacked next to the Clorox bottles.

Next, a small pile of pocket-size white Styrofoam boxes. We looked for a trigger—none—so we opened these first.

There were little test tubes inside with screws at each end of the test tubes. Each test tube had a different-colored liquid inside of it. The tubes were held inside the Styrofoam by clips. On the clips were stamped numbers:

"Ten seconds."

"Twenty seconds."

"Thirty seconds."

"Forty-five seconds."

"Sixty seconds."

I took one out and looked at the screw. "I wonder where this fits?"

I handed Thompson a claymore mine. "See if it screws in here." And Thompson began screwing the blue vial from the "ten seconds" clip. The frightened scream was mine. I was timing him, and he had already spent seven seconds and the vial threads were only halfway in. I didn't think he could screw it all the way in in the three seconds left. I wondered who had tested this device in the states. Charlie Three-Fingers?

"Which one you want us to use, Captain?" Quiet Voice asked.

"Who gives a shit?" said Lieutenant Powell, such a philosopher.

"Let's use the black one. It will give us time to get behind the sandbags." Everyone looked at me. Move the captain up a notch.

Setting a claymore on top of the berm, screwing in the black test tube, and then slipping and sliding back to the sandbags is not easy in the monsoon. But it took less than sixty seconds.

We waited much longer than that.

Finally Pecker, the camp dog, walked over to check out the claymore.

Boom!

Fortunately for Pecker, he was not in front of the claymore when it went off. Unfortunately, he was behind the claymore, which has a backblast kill radius of fifty yards.

All we found was his nose.

"These things happen." Spec. 7 Thompson trying to console us there.

Thompson examined the colored vials.

"It's vibration sensitive! Each vial, when screwed into a claymore, gives different amounts of time before the claymore becomes armed to vibrations."

"What about the Clorox bottles and coffee cans?" I wished Quiet Voice would shut up now and then.

Black Spaghetti spoke. "Let's try them on ambush."

Shotgun groaned.

"What's wrong, Shotgun?" I asked.

"I've never gotten so many toys before." Shotgun wiped away a tear, or maybe a stray strand of spittle. Emotion got to him that way.

"What kind of mission needs this many toys?"

Quiet Voice curled into the corner in a fetal position after asking the question.

Even the ''specialists'' looked worried. Spaghetti took out his billfold and looked at a picture of a beautiful black woman holding a little daughter waving at the camera.

''If you fill your mouth with a razor, you will spit blood.'' His hands shook; he looked at the picture for a long while.

A Long Camping Trip

Can you pronounce these names: plaine des Jarres, Phou Bia, Tha Thom, Borikhane, Soppone, Ang Kahm, Chankeuil Tay, and A Ro?

Neither could Colonel Basshore when he gave us our new assignment. He had flown personally out to the camp to tell us all about it. I remember the day well because it was hot and humid. Of course, every day was hot and humid, so that wasn't hard to remember.

"How come we got to go to places no one has heard of?" Quiet Voice was still in the corner, curled into a fearful little ball.

Spaghetti tried to calm Quiet Voice with a quote: "In a court of fowls, the cockroach never wins his case."

The colonel gave a weak laugh. Shotgun was sitting quietly in the front row of the briefing, cleaning his M-79. The rag with gun oil slid slowly back and forth over the barrel as he stared intently at the colonel. The smell of gun-cleaning fluid excited Shotgun.

Colonel Basshore cleared his throat. "This mission is now sterilized. No personnel hearing what I have to say will be allowed to leave this compound until the mission is completed. Is that clear?" The colonel walked over to our hootch door, looked around, saw nothing except the burnt-out jeep and the decaying carcass of an elephant and a dead North Vietnamese's head stuck on a pike near the front of the camp. One of the Hoa Haos patrols had brought it back and left it as a memento. Of course they never bring back the body. It's too heavy and useless after they eat the liver out of it.

Raw.

They eat the raw liver because that's where the soul is.

It's comforting to know they're religious.

"An old Hmong tribal chief has recently died in Laos. He has been replaced by another elder, who is unknown to us. You will need to make contact with the new chief to ascertain if he is still willing to continue his tribe's relationship with the U.S. We need you to remain on site at an airfield we've been using. Built on tribal grounds with U.S. money and labor, this airfield is important to the war effort."

"How will we know if he's friendly?" Quiet Voice asked.

The colonel glanced at Quiet Voice. He seemed a little miffed at so naive a question, so I answered for him.

"If we're alive after we meet him, he's friendly. If we're dead, he's not."

That didn't seem to help Quiet Voice's misgivings.

Spaghetti tapped me on the shoulder. "If you speak, speak to him that understands you."

He pointed at the colonel, who had resumed talking.

" . . . in short, gentlemen, to secure an airfield near the plaine des Jarres in Laos after assuring us that the new chief is a friendly."

"What for?" Shotgun shifted in his seat.

The colonel flinched and stood behind his aide, who had been holding up a briefing chart. They looked like twin fan dancers. "That's top secret," said the colonel, "and to keep this thing sterilized you will not be told the nature of that mission even after the airfield is secure."

Quiet Voice farted. "You want to know what I think? Since we're going there anyway, and it's an airstrip, what do you want to bet it has something to do with airplanes?"

Shotgun quit wiping his grenade launcher at the mention of airplanes.

The colonel gave an evil grin. "You don't know what airplanes are going to be there."

"So? Why is it important for us not to know?" Quiet Voice was definitely getting out of line.

"Because you may be killed before getting there," Colonel Basshore said, putting him in his place.

"What do we care about the mission if we're dead? Do you think we'll tell God?" Quiet Voice, not staying in his place.

The colonel was turning red, but that changed quickly to white when Shotgun snapped his grenade launcher open and asked, "Are you sure the planes will get there?"

The colonel gave another one of his unique laughs and told Shotgun, "If you do your job, we'll send the planes."

Shotgun loaded the weapon with its large grenade shell—the M-79 looked vaguely like an old blunderbuss—and he snapped it shut. "Can those planes fly to Idaho?"

The colonel stared at Shotgun, eyes bulging with fear, since the question seemed to have serious overtones. He realized a lot depended on his answer.

"I guess . . ." he began in a shaky voice. "If they have enough fuel."

Shotgun lowered the grenade launcher. "We'll take the mission."

The colonel breathed a sigh of relief. I bowed my head and prayed. I had started doing that a lot after the Plain of Reeds. Shortly after the meeting with Colonel Basshore, and hearing the plan about Laos, I began to believe in ghosts, too.

During a typhoon, Colonel Basshore inserted us near A Ro. That was a flaw in the plan. A fly in the ointment. A small plateau des Bolovens mistake; a straight-up-and-down-volcanic-jungle-trails miscalculation; a slog-through-the-headwaters-of-the-Plain-of-Reeds error; in short, a real fuck-up. We were supposed to go in near the plaine des Jarres. A Ro wasn't even close. That's why I began to believe in ghosts.

Only Black, the deal colonel, would have come up with the idea that North Vietnamese would never suspect a helicopter of flying into Laos during a typhoon, especially a helicopter from the delta. I'm sure his ghost whispered to Colonel Basshore that an insertion from the delta into Laos would never be suspected during a typhoon. The idea ranked even with the mobile mortar unit.

Typhoons are Oriental hurricanes. Typhoons circle in one direction. Hurricanes circle in another. If you're being buffeted by one-hundred-mile-an-hour winds, it's hard to tell whether it's a hurricane or a typhoon. Helicopters are not supposed to fly during a hurricane. They weren't made to fly during a typhoon, either. Nobody suspects helicopters of flying during a typhoon because nothing flies during a typhoon. But we did.

Birds don't fly during a typhoon. They know.

First, you can get disoriented.

Which we did.

Next you break radio security to find out where you are.

Which we did.

Then you point a gun at the helicopter pilot and say, "I'd rather walk."

Which Shotgun did.

And walk we did. Slide. Slip. For days. And nights. The hike in the typhoon's rain did wonders for our morale. That and the James Bond thing. I'll tell you about that later.

I sent a radio burst back to Thompson and Powell, who were lucky enough to stay at camp. We were lucky not to have them with us. Thompson's gadgets and Powell's philosophy created too much noise.

If you want to know what "radio bursts" are, carefully place a record on a turntable; now play it at seventy-eight thousand revolutions per minute. That's what a burst sounds like. Three seconds is how long it takes to play something like the *Grand Canyon* Suite. It takes about a tenth of a second to radio a request for help. And less time than that to deny that request.

When I'd asked back at the camp who wanted to stay and who wanted to volunteer for the mission, two people answered.

"Well, somebody has to monitor the radio here at camp," said Spec. 7 Thompson in a microsecond.

"And somebody has to monitor the monitor," Powell added quickly. "Besides," he continued, "all this is meaningless; it's the form we choose to carry out meaningless exercises that tells who we are. And I choose to stay here.'' That took two micros.

Anyway, right now, in the middle of the Laotian jungle, the form we are choosing is an ambush and I want you there. We hadn't had a chance to try out the rest of the gray-box toys—the brown coffee can with a trigger and the clear Clorox bottle—and according to Subervich, the opportunity was now presenting itself. Stand here on the trail with us.

Quiet Voice takes the Clorox bottle from his pack and stares at it. ''How does it work?''

That's easy. I take the bottle from him and stare at it. The top section of the bottle has clear liquid in it. The bottom section has little white pellets in it. Separating the liquid from the pellets is a plastic floor with a ''church key,'' an old-fashioned can opener, poised on a spring above the plastic floor. That's pretty much the same thing Quiet Voice sees.

''You use the can opener to mix the two together,'' I say, and hand it back to Quiet Voice. He isn't impressed.

He stares at the can opener inside the bottle. ''How do I get to it?''

He has a point.

I stare at the can opener floating in the liquid. With a knowing grunt, I pick up a long stick, open the bottle, and begin pushing the stick towards the can opener. The stick dissolves. El problemo.

I shake the bottle. The liquid and beads shake back. Quiet Voice turns the bottle upside down. The liquid and beads follow suit. Finally we all kick the bottle together in frustration. That works.

Quiet Voice walks over and picks up the bottle and brings it back from where we kicked it.

The can opener has shot downward, breaking the plastic floor and causing the liquid at the top to mix with the white beads. Like two Arabs with a magic bottle, we stare as a loud fizzing noise begins. The bottle begins to vibrate. We set it down. Gently.

"Now what?" Quiet Voice takes a step back from the bottle."

I remember the detonator and the little capsules with colored liquid. There are times when inspiration is truly miraculous. God works in mysterious ways his wonders to perform.

"Pour it on the ground," I say in my best command voice.

Quiet Voice is immediately impressed. "Why?"

"You got any better ideas? We can't make them drink it. Now, pour it on the ground. I'll drill a hole in the wet dirt and put a detonator cap in it with one of those colored vials screwed in its top."

"That's supposed to impress the enemy?"

I ignore Quiet Voice's lack of confidence and reach for the vials. Slight problem. When we were running down the trail during the insertion phase of our operation, the little vials shook loose from their clips inside the Styrofoam and are now lying in a heap inside the box.

"Which one for what time?" Quiet Voice sounds stressed.

I can't remember. Pucker factor 9. The little clips that held the vials are still there with their time markings, but the vials aren't talking.

I reach for the black one on top of the pile. I vaguely remember that its time is a long one. I think. Where the hell is Subervich, our mission "specialist"? This is his job.

"Are you sure that's the right one?" Subervich says in a worried voice as he hurries past me feeding fishing line from the trigger on the coffee can now sitting up ahead around a curve in the path ten yards in front of where I'm putting the Clorox juice.

"Can I help you with that heavy line?" says Quiet Voice, who follows him into the bushes, where we'll wait for ambush. I'm all alone as I screw the vial into the blasting cap and shove it into the Clorox-wet ground. I scramble away to join Subervich.

"It took you twelve seconds, so we know it's not the quick one." Subervich, the "specialist."

We lie there quietly, listening to our breathing and the jungle leaves dripping the early morning dew. Shotgun appears by our side and waits. I didn't even know he was near. He's good.

"Where's Spaghetti?" Quiet Voice doesn't sound confident about our chances on the ambush. Why he wouldn't have faith in wet jungle dirt with a blasting cap and colored liquid sticking out of the leaves backed by a coffee can sitting in the middle of the trail with what we hope is the front facing towards the enemy— why he wouldn't have faith in these things was just another irritation.

I promised to tell you about the Bond thing later, and since it is later and we're waiting on an ambush with nothing to do but sweat, I'll tell you what happened.

I'll start at the beginning in the present tense because that's where it stays in my mind:

We are deep in enemy territory, trying to get up to the plaine des Jarres, quiet as mice, and we bump into cattle.

There's an old man with a white wisp of a goatee along with his grandson, a four-year-old, maybe a five-year-old. They're taking the cows over to the neighbor's or over to the next pasture or maybe to market. He's got a bamboo staff to whack the cows on the butt to move them along. The little guy is copying his granddad and is whacking them on the tail with a little stick. They're both laughing. Cowboys. They're the same everywhere you go.

That's why they don't notice us at first. We hide beside the trail and wait for them to pass. Note: Twenty cows cannot walk single file on a trail. They fan out and walk beside each other and on the backs of those trying to hide alongside the trail. It hurts. We stand up, scattering the cattle.

The old man and the young boy freeze.

We freeze.

The cattle stampede.

A situation develops.

"What do you mean, shoot them?" Subervich looks at me. "Why can't we just tie them up and leave them?"

"Because," Shotgun explains patiently, "they've got someone at home waiting for them with dinner. They'll look for them and when they find them tied up, they'll want to know why."

"Small boys make big meals for tigers." Spaghetti musses the hair of the little kid and hands him a candy bar. I remember the photograph of his family. Spaghetti likes kids.

"Can't we take them with us?" Quiet Voice pleads.

We're thirty miles into Laos. We've got another fifty to go. The old man coughs and spits. That noise alone would break any ambush we set up or cause an ambush to be set up against us. Quiet Voice doesn't ask again. He's answered his own question in his mind.

We can't let them go. This is their country. They'll have the troops after us in no time. I look around at the faces of my men. For the first time I can feel the weight of command on my shoulders. It's too damn heavy.

Do you order Shotgun to cut their throats?

What would James Bond do? He goes behind enemy lines. Does he get stepped on by cattle?

No!

Does he cut throats while the camera does a slow pan of the sputtering blood and the choked-off cry?

No!

What would you do? You're free to decide.

Is this a great country or what?

And that's why I'm pissed at James Bond. And that's why we're setting up an ambush. We didn't kill the cows and someone found them wandering around. That someone told somebody and now they're after us.

Quiet! I hear them. Get down.

The first two are coming fast and they have no packs. No packs means someone's carrying their equipment. All they have are guns and ammunition. Probably grenades, too, but I don't see them. These are the point men—the wedge breakers on a football team; the hatchet men in a basketball game. Subervich lowers the fishing line attached to the trigger of the coffee can in case they make it to the vibration-sensitive wet ground. We have no idea what it is supposed to do.

It does nothing.

I glance at Subervich. He holds up five fingers; four, three, two, one finger. We wait. Life waits. It feels like a lifetime, anyway. I know now that other colors are quicker. Great. Quicker for what? Wet ground? It was already wet before I poured the foam on it. Instruction booklet, please.

They pass on, their green fatigues making little swishing noises against the wet plants. Spaghetti follows them, whispering a quote or two:

"You set the trap after the rat has passed.

"He who hunts two rats catches none."

When we pop the ambush, the point men will return.

Spaghetti will be waiting. I hope. He sounds out of shape.

Note: Pour the Clorox after positioning the coffee can.

Reason: When the ground blew up, one of the body parts almost hit the coffee can, knocking it over. The loud explosion surprised the shit out of us. Scared the hell out of the jungle, too. The birds and the monkeys decided not to hang around to find out what the hell had happened. We're talking mass migration, quickly. Hold that ark! A few animals would like to book passage.

"I'll be goddamned!" said Subervich. "That stuff in the Clorox bottle becomes liquid dynamite when it's mixed!"

We duck as body parts begin falling back to earth from the explosion.

The five-by-five hole left in the ground from the Clorox juice took three men with it. I saw six arms, so I assume it was three men. Their five friends, who had been following the unlucky three, begin quickly getting themselves back onto their feet. They know they're in an ambush. There should be a warning label on human beings: "Dangerous when exploded."

When Subervich sees the men on their feet, he jerks the fishing line, and the coffee can explodes outward, towards the five standing men.

I'll never forget the sound two hundred yards of supercompressed double-edged Schick adjustable razor ribbon makes when it is exploding out of a coffee can. Of course, I've never had a need to hear the sound before. Somebody at the Schick corporation sure as hell had a need. They did their part for the boys *over there*. For a slight profit margin. So, for the future Schick ads, let me describe what happened.

The silver ribbon sailed through the air and settled over the young men on the trail like an enraged Slinky. The clatter of weapons being dropped startled us, and we peeked over or around our positions. They were slapping at the razor ribbon and, or course, grabbing it to get it off themselves.

Then their body parts started to fall off.

Not big parts at first—fingers, ears, that sort of thing.

One of them panicked and ran. The Schick ribbon around his neck caught on a tree and jerked tight. He stopped for a moment and ran on, headless. We watched in awe. His body, pumping on adrenaline, took three steps, maybe four, and fell. One of his buddies was screaming and trying to point at his headless friend but the fingers he was pointing with kept falling off. Through it all was the constant sound of crossed sabres and sliding steel, and strange springy sounds.

"A waste of good razor blades!" Shotgun was outraged.

Subervich stood on the trail, looking at the string in his hand and crying. He kicked the empty can from its hiding place and it made an empty-can sound.

Olley, olley, oxen-free!

The CAR-15 sound startled us. It was the first humane weapon fired in the ambush. Shotgun was shooting what was left of the human beings on the trail. We heard two answering shots up the trail—Spaghetti doing his job.

Subervich was saying, "Turn the channel. Turn the channel. See what else is on."

It was good to see he was going to fit right in.

KOA or KIA: Which Is Cheaper?

You can't find God in a triple-canopy jungle. You can't find a goddamned thing in a triple-canopy jungle unless you're a bird, monkey, lizard, or insect. But you're not that lucky—you're a soldier. And that means you've got the bottom. The lucky things that twitter and woof and skitter and howl are on the second and third levels of trees that are growing above you.

Us? We're in the dark—that's the way most intelligence operations are run. It's almost nightfall and we don't even know it because it's been nightfall for the past three hours. No one has said a word about the ambush. We can't say a word about the ambush. We've never shaved that close before. The jungle dark matches our mood.

The men chasing us quit about three hours ago. Once we started into the triple-canopy jungle, they stopped.

"Why did they stop chasing us?" whispered Quiet Voice.

"Because their chase dogs turned on them. Refused to come in here for some reason." Shotgun sounded nervous.

That bothered us. We hadn't known he had nerves.

It's the neutral zone, Captain.

Never mind, Chekhov, warp-speed ahead.

Scotty here, Captain. She won't take much more.

To go where no man has ever gone before.

"Fuck this!" Subervich is wiping something white off his jungle hat. Something that twitters, woofs, skitters, or howls just took a shit above us. Things that live are up there. Things that are dead or dying are down here. Shotgun stops.

"The ground is fuzzy," he says.

"And moving," Spaghetti says.

"And bouncing," says Subervich, cleaning his hat.

"Why is it doing all that?" Quiet Voice says, climbing a vine.

I can see the gray fuzziness from the little stripes of sunlight that filters down. Shotgun sticks his hand in the fuzziness. His hand disappears. It appears. It disappears as the gray reaches up from the jungle floor and roots Shotgun to the jungle. He is part of it. With an effort he jerks his hand clear. It makes a strange sucking noise. Everything that woofs, twitters, skitters, or howls stops to listen.

"Leeches!" Shotgun begins cleaning his hand quickly and jumping. Everyone is jumping to get the crawling mass of gray things off their boots and the bottom of their pants legs. This makes the spongy floor undulate. Two of us fall down.

And get right back up. This isn't the age of mammals. It's the age of worms and insects. You ever seen a worm or an insect on an endangered species list? Point made, okay? There are billions of them. They've been waiting here for eons. Waiting for someone stupid enough to go on a mission through their swamp. Americans.

Why Tarzan used vines.

Why Quiet Voice is climbing one.

Why the little people wouldn't chase us.

We begin running. The floor is still undulating. It's like trying to run on a half-flat trampoline. There's so much decaying vegetation on the floor of the swamp that we can't fall all the way through to the wet darkness below. Just parts of us dip into the water—like our feet, with leeches all over them. Whatever is down there thinks we're fishing. Occasionally a foot is grabbed. Once whatever it is gets the leeches off, it discovers the leather of the boot and rejects it. We aren't wanted even *under* the floor of the rain forest.

There are things in this water the Smithsonian should check out; things Marlon Perkins never talked about on ''Wild Kingdom.''

We break out into elephant grass.

And sunlight.

And fresh air and clouds.

We had forgotten those things.

We can't see the other team. The grass is high.

They can't see us. The grass is high.

Time out.

We decide to eat lunch. If we could build a fire, we would have some LRRP rations. I take one out and look at its silver packaging. It says, ''Shrimp Creole—just add hot water.'' Shrimp—small things that float around in the water; small things like hungry leeches. I look at my boot. Something with teeth has licked it clean, leaving saliva trails. I look at the others. They shake their heads no.

Instead, we all choose C rations. Our little P-38 can openers join in a happy sound as we open up our cans of "Steak, Salisbury, 2 ea.," and dig in.

Gradually, as we try to chew "Steak, Salisbury, 2 ea.," we become aware that a little P-38 is still chattering away, making little squeaking noises.

And none of us are using it. We're all eating "Steak, Salisbury."

We set down our cans and pick up our weapons. Quietly. Shotgun crawls to the edge of the clearing. We let him. When he returns, he holds up ten fingers. No problem. Then closes the hands and reopens the ten fingers twice more. Thirty. My stomach does a little jump, along with "Steak, Salisbury, 2 ea."

The enemy is setting up an ambush. We just got to it at the initial planning phase instead of the finale.

The NVA went around the swamp. We went through it.

"Let's grab some sleep," Shotgun says, stretching and yawning from a prone position. "They won't come in here after us, and we sure as hell aren't going to go anywhere while it's daylight."

I'm not going anyplace where it's dark, either.

There are things that eat you in the jungle.

"We can go back through the swamp." We all stare at Subervich.

"Just a thought," he mutters, stretching out beside us for a well-deserved rest. Spaghetti has his back to me, and I'm picking leeches off his back. Subervich is doing Shotgun and Spaghetti is doing Subervich. I think Shotgun is doing me.

I look back into the triple-canopy jungle. There are monkeys up there grooming each other. They go through the hair of their neighbor's backs and find little insects or whatever and then pop them into their mouths and swallow them.

I hear a crunching sound from Shotgun behind me.

Shotgun chews slowly. I don't turn around.

We sleep with our heads together. Spaghetti has taken the little humm box and stretched the thread in a large circle around us. The box is in the middle of the circle our heads make. If we hear it hum, we'll sit up in four different directions and wait. If we're still alive, somebody will turn off the machine. That hum can be heard two ways.

I send a burst back to Spec. 7 Thompson and Lieutenant Powell, telling them we are not doing well and want to go home.

They send back a burst, asking us, "Are balloons okay?"

Spec. 7 Thompson knows the balloons are not okay. He knows they are standard army-intelligence issue. When you find out what they sent you to find out, you write it down on a slip of paper. Then you tie that paper to a very long string that is coming out of a hole in something that looks like a giant shotgun shell. The end of the string is tied to you somewhere, and you hope there is enough string for the shell to do its job. Confused? Look, it works on the same principal that an astronaut's getting into his capsule on top of the rocket does: he closes the door (you put the shell into the M-79 grenade launcher); he waits (you aim the grenade launcher towards a small hole of daylight three stories above you); they blast him off (you fire the shell); his initial stage falls away (the shell pops open); his booster rockets fire (your little balloon inflates, with your note on the string below it); he sails on off into space and glory (you sit waiting, flying a balloon-kite in the middle of a Laotian jungle, until an L-19 Piper aircraft

"Bird-Dog" flies by and snags your balloon and the message); the astronaut returns to earth with his safety the concern of thousands of people (the Bird-Dog roars off with your message, leaving you with a broken string).

The messenger stays. It's a slow walk in a sad rain home.

You are a run-over puppy.

You are Santa's poisoned reindeer.

You are a wet cat in someone's lap.

You are expendable.

You are shit out of luck.

So you poke holes in the balloons and they have to get the messenger to get the message.

Spec. 7 Thompson is home laughing at his little transmission joke, but we don't answer because if we spend too much time communicating on the radio, vectoring teams of the little people will draw this triangle and we'll be at one of the points on that triangle. Not good. Geometry is not a good science. They'll call the dogs that haven't eaten yet, or haven't been eaten, and it'll be escape–chain-gang time as the dogs bark and we run and run from Mr. Charley, the warden.

See, there are dog teams in the middle of every four kilometers. Think of the Four Corners of New Mexico, Arizona, Utah, and Colorado. Put a dog team there. If a tourist shows up in any of the four states, the dog team is in the middle and ready to go. Get the picture? And it is hard to outrun a dog. Most humans can't. We can.

We have been issued Green Hornets for that very reason. The army issues them to its behind-the-scenes troops as "appetite suppressors." Army doctors tell us to take them during a mission to keep from getting hungry.

Hungry?

Human beings shouldn't be able to outrun dogs.
Eat a Green Hornet and you can outrun cheetahs. Do
thirty hours of work in six minutes. Fly as high as a
chopper in a typhoon and crash as fast as a C-130 in the
same typhoon. Make love faster than a shrew. Read the
Bible, take a shit, write a paper, fall in love—all in
the same minute.

Shotgun has the amphetamines. They're issued
green—standard army color. We don't dare eat them
because we won't be able to sleep or dream. Sleep is
our only vacation from the day—our physical R and R.
Now they're trying to control that. Pop a pill and work
longer for the government.

Shotgun grabbed a handful before we left. He's
been popping them regularly. And is sleeping like a
baby.

Have you ever seen a baby startle?

Don't wake Shotgun up. He's a little on edge.

I spread a rain poncho over me to give the mosqui-
toes a challenge. Shotgun stirs. We sleep head to head
to head to head to head like spokes on a old wheel,
thrown away and abandoned in a field of elephant grass.

What to Do
on Vacation

Subervich had to pee. He told me so.

"I have to pee," he said.

My head was on his right, otherwise he would have told Quiet Voice, who was on his left, and who might have saved his life. Quiet Voice would have answered, "Why are you getting up?"

Which might have made Subervich wake up. I'm sure he had to be dreaming to think he could pee like a normal person. You know, get up in your underwear, walk to the edge of camp, and savor the relief of an empty bladder.

Instead, I mumbled something like "So?" and killed Subervich. He sat up, took off his jungle fatigues, and walked to the edge of the elephant grass. I like to think his last moments were spent with that feeling of emptying himself while watching the birds and monkeys in the trees beginning their day. I like to think he thought he was back in Pennsylvania with some guys on a weekend camping trip, and it was cool in the Allegheny Mountains, and when he finished he would come back and wake us up with fresh coffee and sizzling trout. Or maybe he thought he had a beautiful love sleeping in the tent and when he finished he'd go back and hold her in the cool morning.

But

The machine gun didn't cut him in half. It ripped open the stomach, and his intestines spilled outward to fall on the ground where he'd just peed. At least the ground was partially sterilized. He stared at the intestines steaming in the early morning and made no sense out of what he saw. I know this because I sat up at the first clackclackclack of the machine gun and could look right down the trail he'd made in the elephant grass to where he stood. He was still trying to put his penis back into his shorts when he pitched forward. That's all I saw. It was enough.

That's all I saw because Shotgun had grabbed all his gear and ours and was heading away from the machine gun.

"Now is the time to move because they can't hear us moving," he said. Shotgun was helpful like that. And we followed. We followed because there was nothing else to do for Subervich of Pennsylvania football fame.

That's all I saw. But that's not all we heard.

"Shoot me!"

The scream froze us at the edge of the trees.

"They've got me!"

We turned as one and stared in the direction of the sound. We could hear them talking. They sounded like aliens.

Beam us up, Scotty. Lock in our coordinates.

"For God's sake! Don't leave me."

Randolph Subervich, the football player, was still in the game and wanted out. He was signaling the bench. But we didn't shoot for two reasons: we couldn't see where to shoot and Shotgun was pointing his gun at us, saying, "I'll kill the first man who gives away our position."

He was helpful like that.

Second Day, Second Quarter

We ran until we tripped over the gasoline pipeline. I know what you're thinking: why were we running? Because we wanted to get as far away from Randy's screams as we could. The screams followed us for several hills and valleys in the direction of the plaine des Jarres and I had a feeling they would follow much farther than that, like forever. Close games stay with the athletes.

Quiet Voice tripped over the pipeline first.

"What the fuck is that?" he said, after the clunk of his boot and the thunk of his knee clued us in to put on the brakes. It didn't do any good. We were going downhill at the time on one of those volcanic rain-eroded cliffsides and we couldn't stop.

I closed my eyes. Spaghetti muttered something like, "The cow steps on the calf but does not hate it," and stepped on my nuts as he did a cartwheel over all of us.

Look at the bright side. It might have been a giant

land mine. After exploding Clorox bottles and coffee cans full of razor blades, I was ready to believe anything was possible.

Anything except a two-hundred-mile metal pipeline with petroleum running through it in the middle of Laos. Now, we thought the colonel would want to know the exact location in case someone somewhere needed to see a pipeline full of gasoline in the middle of a jungle. We thought his general would want to know. We thought it was an important tidbit of info for the U.S. So we radioed a burst back to Spec. 7 Thompson telling him to inform the colonel.

That killed one of us. Not then. Later.

We radioed back the location in a long burst, giving command the eight-digit coordinates that would allow the bombs to fall within four hundred feet of the target. "Large petroleum pipeline," the message went. "Suggest arc-light." ("Arc-light" was a secret code word for B-52s. It was a four-year-old word. Everybody, including the enemy, knew it by then.)

The reply was heartwarming and gave poignant meaning to Randy's death, and it made everything clear for all of us. "Do not destroy pipeline. Repeat. Pipeline must stay intact. Continue mission. Send up balloons when mission complete. Do not smoke near pipeline."

"How come we can't destroy this pipeline?" Quiet Voice was flicking his Zippo close to the fumes and squinting his eyes in the growing dark. "Don't these words written here say, 'Property of North Vietnam'?"

We all backed up in case Quiet Voice got more light than he needed.

Spaghetti squatted by Quiet Voice and gave him a bite of his LRRP ration: dehydrated fish with pizza sauce. He slipped a fatherly arm around his shoulder and said, "If one is not in a hurry, even an egg will start walking."

Shotgun kicked the pipeline. The pinging sound

reverberated the entire two hundred miles. It reminded me of the sound ax handles make when they are pounded on metal bleachers. My college, Stephen F. Austin State University in Texas, had a football team called The Lumberjacks. To rattle the opposition, we carried ax handles to the game and beat the handles rhythmically on the metal bleachers.

And suddenly I understood. The pinging sound, Subervich's death, football, America, this war. I understood.

"We can't bomb the pipeline because of the football game."

I drifted away from the rest and studied the large bushes the little people had planted by the pipeline, and admired how they had woven the tops together so that from the air it would look like part of the jungle. Some little gardener had planted these trees, his son had watered them, and the son of his son had built the pipeline, and the son of the son of the son had woven the then-grown trees into a two-hundred-mile biodegradable camouflage net. Well, they didn't have good TV reception in Laos, so they had to stay busy somehow. It was a following-in-the-family's-footsteps kind of thing. I walked back towards the men.

I heard Quiet Voice ask, "What football game?"

"The one we're playing," I said, following Shotgun, who was disappearing up a steep trail that paralleled the pipeline.

If you want to understand the football game, here are the rules:

1. Stay on your side of the fifty-yard line.
2. You cannot play offense.
3. You cannot score.
4. And if there is a fumble, ignore it and play without a ball.

The Third Day Brought Flowers

They were Indians. We knew they were Indians because they wore breechcloths and not much of anything else. And they were delighted to see us, which was a good thing, since there were at least a hundred of them and five of us. Even Subervich wouldn't have helped that much.

A red-toothed old man hobbled from the top of the trail down to us. This was the new chief. Since we were still alive, he was a friendly. His red teeth were the result of chewing betel nut, a mild narcotic that turns the teeth red and the brain on. I wouldn't have noticed his red teeth as much if they hadn't been filed down to sharp points. I wouldn't have noticed the sharp points as much if he hadn't been using a walking stick with a human skull mounted on the top.

"Welcome. Our airfield awaits you. Please call in

the planes. The flowers need to go to market quickly or they will spoil.''

''Flowers? We're shipping flowers now?'' asked Quiet Voice.

''Hey, Captain. We don't look like anybody's idea of flower delivery men,'' Spaghetti said.

I looked at our clothes. He was right.

We were typical representatives of the U.S. government in little out-of-the-way places: clothes rotting off, open running sores from bites on top of bites from insects and other weird, scurrying things that slithered through the hair and dark places on the human body. Right now, they seemed to be in the crotch. They did that around noon of each day.

We stood there with our guns pointed towards the cackling old man, who motioned with his hand, in response to which three women approached with hand-sewn shirts and beaded breechcloths. God works, etc. . . .

''You call and we clean?'' The girls had a point.

We called. They cleaned. Breechcloths aren't bad. While they cleaned the rotten clothes, we wore breech-cloths, a decided improvement. Scurrying things fall out of them. After they brought back our clean, rotten clothes, we begged to trade our uniforms for their breechcloths, but they wouldn't trade. So much for baubles and beads and buying Manhattan.

After calling back to Thompson, who called the colonel, who called the airplanes, we settled down to wait.

We lay at the edge of an airfield hacked from the middle of the first field of elephant grass. Above us circled the rim of an ancient volcano. The wind was cool. It blew through the cracks of the piled rocks stacked on the edge of the airfield. One side of the volcano had collapsed, and a dirt road disappeared down its crumbling slope into the deep jungle. The tribe wouldn't let us go down the road, which was fine with us. Who wanted to go back into the jungle?

A family of loud gibbons was the only enemy in sight. They were just far enough out of reach to be safe. One was playing with his penis or scratching it, like I was mine.

The young women of the tribe had fixed us some dog to eat along with blood pudding from the same dog. It was delicious. But a good meal like that can't make you quit thinking about lost friends. I wished Subervich was still alive to enjoy a good meal.

"Follow the customs or flee the country," said Spaghetti as he reached for another piece of dog. Except for the meal and the volcano, it was like any other picnic. Shotgun was stretched out in the grass, jerking off; Quiet Voice was squatting with the rest of the tribe, putting on face paint; I was trying to kill one of the gibbons with a crossbow. All we needed was a softball game to make it feel like home.

The old man with the red teeth was still cackling as he watched me try to shoot a gibbon. I turned and looked at him, but not for long. He was so ugly.

"What kind of flowers we shipping?" I asked him.

"Our crop. American flyers ride big boom-booms north. North fire big arrows back. Hit metal bird. Pilots float down from sky into here."

He made a large sweep with his hand, indicating the volcano and the rest of the countryside, or else he was brushing away flies from the leftover dog meat. I wasn't sure which.

"We hide pilot until you come get. You take crop to market. We good each other." His grin was so bloody.

I started to ask him what kind of crop it was but

the sound of prop-driven airplanes began echoing off the volcano walls. Two DC-3s and one C-119 came in from the south, circled, and dipped their wings.

The old man's smile turned serious. He motioned to the rest of the tribe and they disappeared down the dirt road into the jungle. Shotgun, Spaghetti, Quiet Voice, and I waited along the airstrip. The noise of the landing planes was deafening.

That's why we didn't hear the old French trucks as they drove onto the airfield behind the landing planes. As the planes taxied to the other end of the airstrip, the French trucks, chipped paint and all, came to a halt and waited. The tribe formed a long chain around the first truck.

The first plane taxied to the human chain and stopped. On the side of the plane was written AIR AMERICA. I was surprised this volcano was one of their routes, but Congress works in mysterious ways, approving some things, disapproving others.

Two tribesmen stood beside the door on the plane and began directing the others to stack what was on the trucks at their feet. On the flat beds of the trucks were large tow sacks the size of cotton sacks. They were full of bright red and white flowers that shook gently when the tribespeople picked them up and began stacking them as directed.

I wanted to whistle "Dixie" but Spaghetti might not have understood.

A man appeared in the door of the plane. He was dressed in civilian clothes and a brightly colored Hawaiian shirt. He was wearing sunglasses, which made as much sense as the Uzi he carried in one hand. With the other he waved at us, giving us a thumbs-up for the war effort.

The Indians began to load the planes quickly. Once

a plane was loaded, its door was closed. The truck then drove off to the side of the runway so that the plane could taxi back around the others to take its place at the end of the line and wait. Each plane contained a man in civilian clothes wearing a brightly colored Hawaiian shirt and carrying an Uzi.

Shotgun was getting edgy.

"Did you bring the tickets?" he asked.

"What tickets?" I shouted over the engines.

"For Idaho!" he shouted back.

"How many Green Hornets you got left?" said Quiet Voice, which was his way of reminding me why Shotgun was on edge.

"None," answered Shotgun.

I tried to smile. "I've got the tickets, Shotgun. When do you want to board?"

"As soon as they finish loading the poppies."

I stared at the few remaining tow sacks waiting to be loaded. Their little red and white tops peeking out at us in all their innocent glory. We were pushing dope for Uncle Sam.

Glancing at Spaghetti, I could see him start to shake.

"Any of your people on heroin back in New York?" Quiet Voice had such tactful ways sometimes. They rivaled Shotgun's.

Spaghetti shook his head. "Even an ant can harm an elephant," he said, and cocked his weapon.

I had a feeling something was going to happen and I didn't have a handle on what. I glanced at the parked planes, whose engines were still running. One of the Hawaiian shirts deplaned and walked towards us. Bad timing.

Second-class Seats

What's eighteen feet long and acts like a pissed-off garden hose?

Okay, so you know it's a king cobra.

We didn't.

There we were, sitting in that cave wondering why the Indians quit chasing us at the foot of the canyon; why the Indians quit chasing us, laughing as they turned away, saying their death gods would take care of us. They'd posted about fifty warriors on the only trail into and out of the canyon, so we couldn't go back. We could hear them ringing their little bells on strings to summon their gods. It was hilarious. You could hear our laughter all the way back to the volcano. We could still smell the smoke of burning airplane fuel.

Shotgun laughed as we climbed the steep, mist-enshrouded canyon. Quiet Voice laughed as we passed small animal bones on the side of the trail. I had trouble getting my breath, so I couldn't laugh, but since I was carrying Spaghetti, that's understandable. Still, I smiled at the stupidity of the natives.

Spaghetti gurgled, which passed for a laugh.

We all stopped laughing when we noticed that the number of bones increased the higher we climbed. The only sound was the echo of us taking the safeties off our weapons.

By the time we found the first "cratch"—storage bins the natives had put together stuffed full of human skulls—we began to convert to the natives' religion.

All except Spaghetti. He was beyond conversion. When you are that close to dying, you have a tendency to stick with the religion that got you there, if you know what I mean. A switch might piss off whatever is waiting on the other side.

I asked Shotgun about it one time before he got too drunk. "What happens when we die?"

"No problem," he answered. "We won't know if we're being punished or rewarded, since the only way we could know that would be if our senses came with us. But hearing, seeing, feeling, smelling, and tasting are attached to the body. It rots."

He told that to Lieutenant Powell, too, and Powell locked himself in his hootch for a week. Philosophical jealousy, we guessed.

At the top of the valley there was nothing but a steep cliff with a huge cave carved out of the base. There was a giant stone Buddha with vines growing all over its face and down to the large folded legs. There were no birds, no little animals—nothing alive except us in this canyon.

There were a lot of little cratches.

There was nowhere else to go.

What do you think, Spaghetti?

"Gurgle, gurgle."

Why was I carrying Spaghetti?

I was carrying Spaghetti because the French make cheap rubbers. Gasoline eats through cheap ones quicker than quality ones. Still confused? Let's start with the guy in the Hawaiian shirt who'd been walking towards us.

The guy's name was "Smith" and he lived "somewhere" in the South and he'd worked for Air America for a "few" years. The scars on his face and hands said the airline treated their employees poorly.

He knew our names.

He knew where we were from.

He knew our families.

He knew our brand of coffee.

CIA.

"Smith" wanted us to know what a great job we'd done. He also wanted to know if he could speak to Shotgun privately. Quiet Voice, Spaghetti, and I watched them walk back to the center of the dirt runway and have a small discussion. At the end of the runway sat the airplanes, engines ready for takeoff. Across the runway from us, sitting around and on the old French trucks, was the Laotian tribe. For some reason they reminded me of a gang of toughs waiting at the corner for little kids with lunch money.

Quiet Voice and I took off our safeties, joining Spaghetti: we were good kids with lunch money. Then Smith handed something to Shotgun, who put whatever it was into his pocket and walked away towards one of the French trucks. Smith walked over to us as Shotgun gathered a crew and disappeared into the jungle. Smith stopped about twenty feet from us, staying between us and the airplanes. His Uzi hung loose (but in perfect position) on its strap under his right arm.

Have gun. Will travel.

"You need to worry about that Shotgun, boys,"
said Smith, smiling.

He didn't have to tell us that. That was old news.

"We need some gas for the planes and there's a
little storage place near here, but the 'skins can't read
English, so Shotgun said he'd get the right octane for
the planes. Couple of barrels per plane and we'll be on
our way. Shit, the son of a bitch asked if I had any
rubbers." Smith laughed. "Where in the hell is he
going to get any pussy in the jungle?"

Shotgun and sex. That was news?

"I gave him what I had." Smith winked at us with
a scarred eyelid. "They're different colors. Got 'em in
Paree."

"Did Shotgun mention Idaho?" asked Quiet Voice.

Smith wrinkled his brow. "Idaho? Why in the hell
would he mention Idaho?" He chuckled. "You beanies
got a real weird sense of humor."

"Are you sure he didn't mention anything about
Idaho?"

"Look. I asked him to go get some gasoline for the
airplanes. We've got some customers for the gasoline in
Thailand. Got to make a living. You know how it is.
Told him to take some of our boys with him. Said he'd
be happy to get us some fuel. Boys. Wait a minute."
Smith frowned a little. "Shotgun's not queer, is he?"

We shrugged our shoulders. We hadn't yet found
the right classification for our friend.

Something was wrong. If there was no Idaho for
Shotgun, then:

Shotgun helping them load fuel was like Napoléon
shining Wellington's boots;

Superman and Lex Luther going into partnership.

So we waited nervously for what seemed an eternity until Shotgun drove back onto the runway with a truck full of fifty-gallon drums of gasoline rocking in the truck bed. He was alone.

We saw Smith glance from the truck to the dark forest.

We saw Smith touch his weapon nervously.

Monkey see, monkey do. We did the same.

But nothing happened. Shotgun went to each plane, carefully rolling the barrels of gasoline up the platforms provided from inside the doors, where other Hawaiian-shirted men in dark glasses rolled the barrels back against the crop of poppies. Then he drove the old French truck back alongside the other trucks and parked it.

The tribesmen were looking back at the jungle. Shotgun began walking across the runway towards us. The natives' gestures were becoming more animated. A few of them made threatening moves towards Shotgun with their bows. Shotgun began to trot. He was still smiling.

It was hot in the middle of that volcano. The steam rose from the ground and I wiped away the sweat. Smith was trying to watch us and the trotting Shotgun at the same time. It couldn't be done. Smith was as nervous as the natives, one of whom had gone over to the bed of the truck and was now holding a bloody breechcloth. This just made them more nervous. Shotgun broke into a run just as one of the Hawaiian shirts dropped a barrel and held his hand out the door, hollering for Smith. His hand was red, smeared with blood.

Smith made a decision and whirled to meet Shotgun, whom he evidently considered the greater danger. That embarrassed us. There was only one of Shotgun and three of us, but, to tell the truth, I would have done the same. After all, Smith was a pro.

Shotgun hit the runway and rolled right. Smith shot a burst low and to the left: right action, wrong direction.

One of the planes taxied by, lifted into the air, and promptly disintegrated. So did the relative calm in the volcano. Smith jerked his head upward towards the explosion. The natives froze in their angry gestures towards Shotgun. Other Hawaiian shirts looked out from the doors of the other planes.

We just ducked.

I'm not sure if Shotgun's bullet hit Smith first or if Spaghetti's did. I saw him stagger towards us, then back towards Shotgun. Through the hole in Smith's chest, we could see Shotgun waving us towards the rocks on the floor of the volcano.

Spaghetti managed to say, "One does not slaughter a calf before its mother's eyes," which makes me think Shotgun shot first and Spaghetti's move was just a reaction. I'm no expert. But that's what Spaghetti managed to say before one of the Hawaiian shirts from one of the two planes left on the ground shot him in the arm and the lower leg.

They were lucky shots, but when you're using an Uzi with extra bullets and you're firing from a taxiing airplane, you get lucky sometimes. Or unlucky. Just ask the first plane—the one whose pieces were falling like shrapnel all around us.

The first bullet knocked Spaghetti's leg forward so it looked like a kicker kicking a ball, the second spun him around from the blow to his arm. There was a stunned look on his face; then one of relief that it had finally happened.

A lot of professional soldiers know what I mean.

We would have helped Spaghetti a little faster if we hadn't been dodging crossbow arrows from the

Indians across the runway. And pieces of the blown airplane. And bullets from the other planes.

Shotgun grabbed Spaghetti on the run, picking him up, ignoring the screams, and threw him to me.

"Follow me. I'll provide cover!" he said as he ran by, firing wildly in all directions. Gibbons were dying, Asiatic Indians were dying, and one black sergeant from Harlem was dying, too, for the wounds were large and the blood was spurting a long way into the air. Not as high as the airplanes but high enough. It wasn't a time to panic. It was more like a time for sheer terror.

I calmly asked Shotgun what he would suggest.

That's a lie.

I screamed at the fading back of Shotgun, "Shotgun! They're just Indians with crossbows. What are you afraid of?" Spaghetti was heavy; otherwise I would never have dared to talk to Shotgun like that.

"The grenade I put inside the gasoline barrels might go off on the planes while they're on the runway. Cheap rubbers!" he shouted over his shoulder as the planes began to taxi towards me and the wounded Spaghetti. I looked at the wounded man. Then I thought about burning airplane fuel all over my body.

Spaghetti wasn't so heavy.

I threw him over my good shoulder. Quiet Voice and Shotgun provided covering fire until I got to the rocks. The other arm didn't work too well with an arrow stuck in it. "The natives were restless" had to be the understatement of the century.

The rocks weren't Fort Apache, but they were okay for the moment. They were lovely when I dived behind them with Spaghetti.

As we took a breather and listened to arrows clink off the rocks around us, I checked on Spaghetti's wounds. Now, in the movies, there's a neat little hole that can be bandaged during the commercial, and the hero is ready to wave good-bye with the wounded arm by the end of the show.

And there were two neat little holes where the bullets went in: one in the right biceps, the other just below the knee. Where the bullets tumbled out is the part they don't show on television.

Spaghetti was missing his right triceps from the elbow to the shoulder, and the leg dangled below the knee from a couple of lucky tendons that had been out of the way of the crazed bullet. From the front the leg looked okay, like a theater flat covered with a canvas. From behind, the leg looked like a theater flat from behind: hollow, with a few boards holding things together. Spaghetti grabbed my arm. "Not to know is bad; not to wish to know is worse." Actually, he didn't grab my arm. He grabbed the arrow in my arm, jerking it out.

This got my full attention—and Quiet Voice's. He began bandaging my arm. I looked at Spaghetti and then at Quiet Voice. Quiet Voice shook his head.

The army manual says that it is necessary to lie to a wounded soldier to keep him from going into shock and dying. Shock was what Spaghetti needed. Sometimes it's necessary to hurry death along.

"You're in a world of hurt, Spaghetti," I said, holding his head in my lap.

He closed his eyes and smiled. "The end of an ox is beef, the end of this lie is grief."

I pretended I understood: I nodded. I gave him that false reassurance all the living give to the dying—the reassurance we all understand.

What I really wanted to say was something else, like: Why the fuck are you dying? If you die, then I can die, and that's not what I really need to think about while

I'm crouching in a volcano somewhere on the other side of the fucking world.

That's what I wanted to say; instead, I gave his good arm a reassuring pat.

The arrows had stopped falling some time before, and Quiet Voice and Shotgun were peeking around the rocks towards the runway.

"What are they doing?" I asked as I brushed away the flies from Spaghetti's drying blood. I remembered the old chief doing the same thing with his dog pudding. There are a lot of strange memories in war.

If you live long enough to remember.

Something I desperately wanted to do.

"Waiting and counting their money," said Shotgun.

"Why are they doing that?" asked Quiet Voice.

"They get paid for maintaining the runway, loading the plane, and protecting the pipeline." Shotgun reloaded his grenade launcher. "When we found that pipeline, we were as good as dead, anyway."

"What the hell are you talking about, Shotgun?" I asked, brushing away more flies.

"That was a corporate pipeline running out of somewhere and going somewhere, and the North Vietnamese sure as hell didn't build it and the U.S. sure as hell is not going to bomb it—and guess where it stopped?"

Spaghetti managed to shrug his good shoulder as if to say, "Beats me."

"In the jungle where I went to pick up fuel. We're running drugs now." Shotgun said this with a note of wonder in his voice. "We're supplying heroin to the world, and these Indians and the Hawaiian shirts are getting rich off a mission that's sanctioned by both sides!"

Quiet Voice asked in a low voice, "What sides?"

"The NVA and the U.S. know it's there. Hell, they camouflaged the whole pipeline."

Change of game plans here.

Both teams versus the referees.

The fans sit blindfolded, feeling their ticket stubs.

And we're climbing towards the broadcast booth.

"This is a war and America doesn't work with its enemies," I protested as Shotgun looked at me like a teacher discovering a slow student.

"Their weapons cost money just like ours do. Somebody has to pay for all the machinery both sides use. What better way to get untraceable cash for war supplies than drug money from drugs sold in the U.S.?" Shotgun rubbed a weary hand over his eyes.

"But why kill us?" moaned Quiet Voice.

"Because we know. When Smith said 'our boys,' I realized these Indians were mercenaries, not natives to the area. Besides, when is the last time the CIA gave a shit about a downed pilot?"

"Then why send us in the first place?" I wasn't sure I wanted to hear the answer.

Shotgun leaned back but kept his hand over his eyes. He answered in a voice as flat as a hanging judge's voice. "That's what I couldn't figure out. It came to me after I killed the last guy helping me with the gasoline in the jungle. We weren't supposed to get this far. Nobody thought we were crazy enough to go through the swamp where the leeches were. That's why we busted the damn ambush."

He was silent but I had to know. "So?"

He took his hand away from his eyes and looked at me. I could see his pupils and there were infinite circles behind those. His lips drew thinner. I wondered what the hell was so funny.

"We were the perfect cover. Colonel Basshore

thought we were checking on a new chief. If they had killed us, someone would have told Basshore that the chief was not a friendly and the airfield would have had to be closed. This airport would be off the maps and forgotten. These people are looking ahead to the end of the war. They were setting things up so no one would ever look for this airfield again.''

''Why didn't the chief just kill us when he saw us?''

Shotgun reached over and held up the holey balloon on my belt. ''They didn't know whether or not you'd sent out the message about the pipeline. They intercepted the radio message but they didn't know about the little balloon.''

Shotgun sighed. ''Colored rubbers. What will they think of next? If Smith hadn't had any, I was going to use the rubber from one of the old French tire tubes. Hell, it was our only chance. I used one red rubber on the first grenade, two blues on the second, and a white, blue, and red on the third. Pulled the pin and plopped those grenades into the barrels of fuel. Course, I had one pretty yellow one left over.''

''Why rubbers?'' I asked, not daring to ask where the yellow one had gone.

''Gasoline eats through the rubber, releasing the grenade handle. The rubber was just so weak the gasoline ate through it quicker than it should have.''

''You've done this before, Shotgun?'' Quiet Voice asked, obviously impressed.

''Once in Angola, once in Africa.''

''What were we doing in Africa?'' I asked.

Shotgun didn't hear me because the second plane exploded at the lip of the volcano and the echo of the crash reverberated on the walls of the volcano and inside the walls of our heads. So I repeated the question but he shook his head.

The roar of the last airplane lifting into the air drowned out our conversation. We rolled over and watched the plane clear the volcano and disappear into the west.

The natives stood in the middle of the runway and waved the plane away as it faded off into the afternoon sun.

"Shit!" said Shotgun, "I wanted to see the last one explode. Those fireballs can be pretty."

Quiet Voice brought us back to earth. "If the natives are going to kill us, why are they going back to the trucks?" He was standing.

Shotgun looked around the rocks. "Because this is their country. They know we've got only one way out of here—the way we came—and they'll know where to set up an ambush. And don't think the Hawaiian shirts aren't going to have some kind of backup. That last plane had time to radio a message to both sides. We, gentlemen, are up shitosky creek!"

Spaghetti gave a little rattle of cough.

Quiet Voice pointed at Spaghetti. "What about him?"

"Can he walk?" Shotgun said, watching the natives climb into their French trucks and drive back into the jungle.

Sure, he can walk.

He can hop on one leg through Laos.

A Guinness-world-record hop.

Shotgun took my rifle. "You carry him, I'll cover." As he was fitting Spaghetti onto my back in a fireman's carry, I couldn't help but ask why we were taking Spaghetti with us. He was heavy and would die anyway.

This may sound cold, but war brings out the practicality in a person.

"As long as he's alive, his body will keep pumping blood. That will allow us to make some distance."

"Why?" I asked, adjusting Spaghetti.

"It gives them a blood trail to follow at a safe distance. It's a lot easier than tracking healthy humans with guns. They know we'll travel slow and that it's just a matter of time. When we bury him, that's when they'll attack." Shotgun peered around the rock and fired a grenade at the few remaining guards, driving them back away from the runway.

"Hopefully, by then we'll have found the NVA guys who killed Subervich. They'll help us." With that cryptic saying, he dashed out from behind the rock, firing with both rifles, clipping the leaves off the jungle trees and killing some gibbons in the process.

"Why would we want to find the NVA?" asked Quiet Voice as we sprinted across the abandoned airfield and down the road to the bottom of the volcano, where Shotgun waited.

"Shotgun's got a plan," I said, trying to sound convincing.

"Like his Plain of Reeds–river plan that got us those blood flukes?" asked Quiet Voice.

I wish he hadn't brought that up.

A Zoological
Lesson

And that's why we were in the cave with the giant
stone Buddha. It was twilight and there was no noise
whatsoever. There was a little wind blowing two vines
at the mouth of the cave.

"I wonder what killed all these people?" said
Quiet Voice, throwing rocks at a skull that made a
hollow thunk sound every time he scored a direct hit on
the white forehead.

"Don't sweat it," said Shotgun, sweating.

"Gurgle." Spaghetti.

"Where do snakes like to live?" asked Quiet Voice.

I looked at him, wondering what brought that up.
"They like to den together in caves during the cold
season," I said. "They lie in heaps so their body heat
can keep them all warm. Then as the seasons warm they
come out of the cave to bask in the sun."

"Are they hungry when they come out of the cave?"

I laughed. "Wouldn't you be if you hadn't eaten all winter?"

"How come those two large vines keep swaying?" asked Quiet Voice. "Why are those vines swaying but the treetops aren't?"

Quiet Voice had a point but I couldn't dwell on it long, since I was changing Spaghetti's blood-soaked bandages. We were safe here and that was all that mattered.

"What kind of vine has a big hood that flares out and vibrates with other vines?"

I glanced at Quiet Voice, weary of his questions. "I don't give a fuck what kind of vines they are."

"Well, you should because there's about twenty of them right behind you and Quiet Voice," said Shotgun, real quiet.

And there they were. King cobras don't like to be disturbed when mating. Least, these didn't. The natives had been making human sacrifices to them for so long, they had no respect for us at all. Religious customs and the blood from Spaghetti made them hungry.

Shotgun fired a smoke grenade, which just made them angrier. We couldn't fire our rifles for fear of careening bullets in the cave. They would be as hard to dodge as—well, as hard to dodge as a striking cobra.

The snakes began to chase us.

Slither, slither.

Stop.

Rise.

Scramble, scramble.

Slither, slither.

Stop.

Rise.

Stumble, stumble.

The first three lines describe what king cobras do

when chasing their prey. They slither, they stop, they rise like reptilian periscopes, view the landscape, then follow. In this case they followed us as we scrambled and stumbled down the canyon.

Going back down the trail was easier than climbing it.

"He that diggeth a pit shall fall into it; and whoso breaketh a hedge, a serpent shall bite him," mumbled Spaghetti.

We shot by the guards like shit through a goose. It was nothing personal, but if they hadn't turned and raised their guns to kill us, they might have seen the snakes, which were coming fast.

Whoops! More skulls for the cratches.

You'd think that would satisfy most gods. Not these. The screams of their ecstatic worshippers covered our rapid descent back to the safety of the triple-canopy jungle. It also covered the sound—slither, slither—of the pursuing cobras.

I could hear Quiet Voice's heavy breathing behind me.

"Don't those snakes ever quit?" Pant, huff, wheeze. "I mean, how far are they going to chase us?"

"I know this sounds crazy," I said, gasping—Spaghetti was not getting any lighter despite the blood loss—"but what if they work in relays? I mean, there were a lot of snakes, and popping smoke really pissed them off."

Shotgun had disappeared ahead into another triple-canopy jungle. I didn't think I wanted to see another jungle, but times and snakes changed a person's opinions.

As do Indians.

The arrows just missed Quiet Voice as he sprinted by me. I saw my cover disappear after Shotgun. I wasn't worried about the arrows. Spaghetti covered my back.

Then I heard Shotgun: "Don't worry about the arrows! It's those two snakes right on your heels you've got to worry about."

I know king cobras are territorial, but where does their territory end?

Probably Idaho.

Question: What do you call a triple-canopy jungle that has been bombed with Agent Orange?

Answer: White sticks.

The triple-canopy rain forest changed from a verdant green to a ghostly white-powdered deadness. We felt like three-year-olds crawling over Olympic-size hurdles of fallen trees. How long had we been gone? A week? Two weeks? A day? Where was the pipeline? We felt like we were in a giant pick-up sticks game.

"At least the snakes have quit chasing us," I said, trying to break the uneasy feeling that had come over everyone.

Maybe it was the dead animals all around us.

Their little feet pointed up towards the sky.

Maybe it was the dead plants all around us.

Their roots pointed up towards the sky.

Maybe it was the dead NVA all around us.

Their hands, frozen into claws, pointed up towards the sky.

"Wonder where this stuff came from?" said Quiet Voice.

We all looked up at the sky and back at Quiet Voice.

He looked at the dead bodies pointing up.

"That's a stupid question, isn't it?" he said.

"Shit!" said Shotgun, kicking a dead NVA. "We needed these assholes and they had to go and die on us."

"Shotgun," I said, "I'm a little unclear on why

you think these people would help us. Can you shed some light on that?''

He bent down and brushed some fine white powder off the pocket of a green uniform that still had a body in it. He drew out a Hershey candy bar. Unwrapping it and blowing white dust off it, he looked at me. ''They're soldiers like us. I was going to shoot a couple to make them chase us back to the pipeline. When they found the pipeline, they would have had to join up with us.'' He took a bite of the candy bar and offered some to us. We declined.

''Why?'' asked Quiet Voice.

''Because the poor NVA soldiers would have reported it to their superiors, who would have ordered the same Hawaiian shirts looking for us to stop by and kill these guys, too. Two birds with one stone, or machine-gun bullet, so to speak.''

It wasn't a bad plan. Just crazy. But so was a protected pipeline in the middle of a Laotian jungle.

''If this stuff killed all these things, won't it kill us, too?'' Quiet Voice was trying to tiptoe over a seven-foot hurdle. It couldn't be done. I paused while filling up my canteen with some brackish-looking water from a bomb crater; he had a point. I put in the water purification tablet and shook the canteen, knowing we would be drinking poison but knowing it was wet poison, and drinking wet poison was better than dying of thirst.

I think.

''It won't kill us as fast as those cobras over there,'' said Shotgun quietly.

Guess who was back.

In a Field
of Flowers

The good news is that we are past the deadly white forest. The bad news is that we are crawling on our bellies in a poppy field, hiding from the Cobra. Not the cobras; they're somewhere in the field of poppies, hiding, too. Right now, it's every reptile for himself. If we move, the Cobra gunship will find us. If we stay still, the cobras will find us.

The Cobra gunship is a deadly little machine. It's about as wide as a small couch and as long as two long couches, and it will definitely put you to sleep. The rear cockpit has room for only one pilot, carefully tucked inside like a race-car driver. There was a space for another pilot directly in front of the first, but in 1969 in order to save money, it was usually empty. That pilot had been replaced by two sandbags for balance. Armor shields on both sides of the pilot's seat protect all but the head. Everything outside the cockpit is designed to blow your head off.

A modern knight with body armor and great weapons.

I look at my tattered uniform. I feel like a peasant.

Well, Stanley, this is another fine mess you've gotten us into.

You choose: If a cobra bites you, the poison attacks the nervous system and you die in about sixty seconds, give or take a few venomous jerks. If a Cobra gunship finds you, its Vulcan will fill you full of holes in about ten seconds and there will be no jerks at all. If the Vulcan misses, there's always the fully automatic 40mm grenade launcher called a Honeywell, and if that doesn't do the job, there are always the rockets mounted in their rocket pods alongside the gunship.

Choice made? All right, we stay still.

"There's no markings on that son of a bitch," said Shotgun. "It's as black as Spaghetti."

We could hear it gridding off the huge poppy field. It made whispering passes: whish, whish, whomp, whomp, whish, whish, whomp, whomp. It would eventually make a pass over us, too. We knew it was just a matter of time.

The whishing sound was the noise suppressor on its engine. Only the top secret helicopters in Vietnam had them. Only the best pilots were allowed to fly them.

Great.

The whomp, whomp was the sound of a burst from the Vulcan. Its bullets strike the ground at about the same time, moving at about the same velocity. I remember reading somewhere that the Vulcan cannon could put a bullet in every square inch of a football field in one minute.

Great.

Only the CIA and Special Operations were allowed to have the unmarked black helicopters. They were used mainly on "termination" assignments of questionable legality.

Great.

We lay under a bed of red poppies listening to the sound of the helicopter at the far end of the field and watching the ground for slithering snakes.

"What if one of the cobras bites me in the balls?" asked Quiet Voice.

"Then you're as dead as Spaghetti," said Shotgun, parting the flowers and watching the helicopter.

"Spaghetti's not dead," I said, checking his pulse. "At least not yet."

And he wasn't. The wounds were still oozing blood, which was good because it kept the area clean. Shotgun had mentioned, back in the white rain forest, to let the flies lay their eggs in the wound, since the maggots would eat the dead flesh and keep gangrene from setting in. He was knowledgeable about things like that.

If only the flies had lived through Agent Orange.

Which they hadn't.

But we had.

At least until now.

I kept pouring sulfa powder into the wounds and using strips of my shirt—what was left of it—to keep the gauze pads in place. Shotgun crawled over to the dying man and whispered in his ear. It was a rare compassionate moment for all of us. I saw Spaghetti nod when Shotgun looked into his face for an answer. Shotgun cradled Spaghetti's head in his arms. It reminded me of that Italian statue—some mother cradling her dying son.

This was a pietà in fatigues.

There are a lot of those in war.

The Cobra gunship lifted up and away from the field and disappeared over the trees.

"Is it gone?" asked Quiet Voice.

"It's low on fuel. It'll go to the Indians, refuel,

and be back on station in a couple minutes," said Shotgun.

"Why don't we run?" I asked, beating Quiet Voice to the question.

"Look over in the tree line surrounding the field. Our friends from the volcano."

In the jungle that surrounded the poppy field, small brown shadows moved quickly into position. Not only were they angry about our having taken their gods from their sanctuary—not by choice, but try to tell them that; not only were they angry at our having destroyed the planes taking their farm produce to market; they were now angry because we'd chosen to hide in their field of new poppies, destroying their source of revenue.

Some people are just bad news.

That's us.

Shotgun crawled away and disappeared into the flower field. In a minute he came back with two large tree branches tied to his legs. He untied the branches and passed them over to us along with the leather strings he'd taken from his boots. He crawled over to Spaghetti and whispered something in his ear. Spaghetti grabbed his arm and said something back.

"What did he say?" asked Quiet Voice.

"He said, 'Ignore that man behind the curtain, just listen to the wizard.'" Shotgun began to unbutton what was left of Spaghetti's shirt.

I looked at Quiet Voice. He looked at me and shrugged. Some people make no sense when they're dying. Some people make no sense while they're living: Shotgun, for example—

"Take your bootlaces off and strap Spaghetti's arms to the shorter branch. I'll tie the longer branch to the shorter one and we'll make a cross. Tie his legs to the longer branch and we'll raise him up when the Cobra comes back.'' Shotgun took Spaghetti's shirt off and crawled back into the flowers, taking the shirt with him.

See what I mean.

Whish, whish. Whomp, whomp.

Cobra was back.

Somewhere in the flowers we heard Shotgun's voice:

''Fucking snakes!''

It wasn't the best of times.

Necessity
Is a Mother

At the far end of the field the Cobra gunship had stopped and turned to face Spaghetti and was hovering there, trying to understand the meaning of a black man hanging on a makeshift cross in a field of poppies in the middle of Laos.

"How can a dying man weigh so much?" Quiet Voice was acting as a counterbalance at the base of the cross and was trying to keep Spaghetti from twisting. A trickle of blood ran from Spaghetti's wounds down the cross, making the task slippery and more difficult.

I was on my stomach in front of the cross, looking for Shotgun. He hadn't returned since the little shout about the snakes. There was a knot in my stomach as tight as the knots that held Spaghetti to his branches.

His good arm was tied at a right angle, palm up, making him look like a scarecrow cop halting birds from landing in his field. His head hung on his chest, and except for an occasional deep breath, there was no sign of life. We weren't able to tie his ankles to the vertical branch, since there wasn't enough left to tie below the knee, so we had crossed his legs at the knees and tied them. He was no Jesus, but crucifixion was a dying art form, anyway. We'd done the best job we could under the circumstances.

The helicopter began making its way towards Spaghetti, in cautious swaying movements. For some reason it did not fire. Where was Shotgun? He had to tell us his plan. We still didn't know what it was. We had Spaghetti on a cross and now what? The Cobra swayed closer.

Surely Shotgun wasn't dead. I kept looking for the flowers to bend and sway to tell me Shotgun was coming back, but—nothing. I could see the pilot now as the Cobra hovered past me. His eyes were glued to Spaghetti. He was having trouble comprehending the why of it all.

Weren't we all?

As the Cobra hovered in front of the cross, its blades flattened the flowers around the base, exposing Quiet Voice. It also exposed me, but since I was lying under the belly of the helicopter, the pilot couldn't see me. He glanced at Quiet Voice huddled at the base of the cross, his arms wrapped around the branch, trying to keep it from falling in the rotary wind. The Cobra was five feet off the ground.

Even the king cobras could get higher than that.

The pilot raised his head and stared at Spaghetti. Slowly, Spaghetti raised his head and looked with dying eyes into the bubble of the chopper at the helmeted pilot. He smiled, and with the good hand, the one tied at a right angle to his body, he closed down all the fingers into a fist—all except the middle one.

It was the bravest act I've ever seen.

It wasn't the smartest act; I saw that later.

But it was the bravest.

The Vulcan snapped from pointing downward at the crouched Quiet Voice to a direct position at the hanging Spaghetti. The burst was deafening to me—I was lying under the chopper—and lasted for about ten seconds. That was enough to cover me with spent cartridges and eliminate Spaghetti's body and the branches he was tied to from the world.

The bullets made, well, spaghetti out of Spaghetti.

He didn't have time to feel a thing.

His death was a small, green victory for the poppies.

The cannon began to shift downward. Quiet Voice was next. I reached up with my Randall and cut the electrical cord that positioned the cannon, stopping its downward movement. This distracted the pilot, who began flicking the toggle switch that operated the cannon.

While he was looking at his instrument panel, I jumped on the left skid of the Cobra, tapped the window with my rifle barrel, and pointed my rifle at the pilot. I screamed several names at him for killing Spaghetti, but deep in my heart I was grateful to him for taking Spaghetti out of his misery.

Fortunately, he couldn't hear me because of the rotary noise, but he felt the weight when I stepped on the skid. He gave me a scornful glance, then pointed to a decal on the window. I bent forward to read what it said.

BULLETPROOFING BY HUGHES AIRCRAFT CORP.

One should look before one leaps.

He pointed to his other window, which was open, and shook his head; his way of saying, "Nice try. Good plan. Might have worked if you had gotten on the other skid."

He bent forward and flicked a toggle switch. I squinted through the window, almost reading what it said. ROCKET PODS...I glanced around to see where they were. The pod was not more than ten feet from me, its six rocket heads pointing at my middle. For some reason they reminded me of wasp larvae inside their combs.

And I had to go and jump on the nest.

I couldn't jump off the skid because then Quiet Voice and I would be dead. He'd just fly up to about fifty feet and fire the rockets and the Vulcan. At least this way Quiet Voice could try to run.

I glanced down at Quiet Voice. He hugged what was left of the cross, waiting with his head bowed.

Sorry, Quiet Voice. It seemed like a good idea.

The pilot, like the queen wasp, turned his bughead towards me and gave me a thumbs-up sign. I'm sure he was smiling beneath that opaque visor but I couldn't tell. I saw the rocket pods rotate in the chamber. I watched in horror as the pilot reached towards a switch that had my name written all over it.

If he missed at this distance, he had five more tries.

Hit the cowboy and win a Kewpie doll.

Even Ray Charles couldn't miss.

I felt the Cobra give a jerk and for a moment thought the first rocket was taking an inordinately long time to travel the ten feet from the pod to my belly. When I opened my eyes, the pilot had one hand up in the air. It was the hand that was reaching for the switch. This didn't disturb me, since I was still alive.

Glancing up from the pilot, I saw Shotgun on the opposite skid from me, his grenade launcher pressing tightly against the helmeted pilot, his arms deep inside the open window on the other side, one hand still carrying a blood-stained, balled-up shirt, his only memento of the departed Spaghetti.

Following Shotgun's orders, which I couldn't hear, the pilot let his window down on my side.

I reached inside and grabbed a pistol hanging next to the pilot's seat and threw it out. The pilot had his hands on the stick and seemed like a robot under Shotgun's control.

Shotgun had that effect on people.

Quiet Voice walked around to Shotgun's side and Shotgun shouted something to him. He nodded and walked around the front of the helicopter and crawled up onto the skid next to me.

"How would you like to fly home?" he said as he reached inside and got a firm grip on the pilot's bullet shield, which surrounded his seat.

"Where are we going to sit?" I asked as I reached inside, feeling for something to hold on to. I was having another one of those bad feelings.

"What makes you think we're going to sit?" Quiet Voice shouted back because the pitch of the rotors had changed to a deep, throaty roar. The pilot had pulled back on his stick and like magic we were three hundred feet above the poppy field.

My hands were cold. It was air-conditioned inside the Cobra.

I wasn't about to put them in my pockets to get them warm.

Up, up, and away.

We were flying "standby."

I could imagine the headlines. "Texas Cowboy Shot in Ass While Flying over Enemy." From where I was hanging, I could glance down at the green jungle and watch little red tracers arc their angry way up towards me and Quiet Voice. Inside the cockpit the pilot had relaxed, knowing Shotgun wouldn't kill him at seven hundred feet above the earth.

We weren't so sure.

Tracers are bullets coated with phosphorus so you can see them at night.

Unfortunately, you can also see them during the day.

Anyway, he'd turned on a little laptop tape recorder and the sounds of Sly and the Family Stone were reverberating off his helmet and outside the window to us.

It went something like, "Na, na, na, na, nana, nana, na, na, na."

It was the number one hit in America at the time.

Speaking of hits, every third bullet was a tracer, so when they arced towards one, one could count (to pass away the time) the number of red tracers and multiply by three to determine how many shots were really being fired at one's ass.

If one was bored.

Which we weren't.

"Did you know they just fired three thousand rounds of ammunition at us?" said Quiet Voice.

Well, at least *I* wasn't bored.

I glanced at the passing forest. We seemed to be headed along the same route we'd taken into Laos. I thought about that being a remarkable coincidence until I realized Shotgun was eyeballing the route from the air because it was the only way he knew to get us home.

So it wasn't long until he saw the herd of cattle still milling around, wondering where the old man and his grandson had disappeared to.

We were back at the scene of the crime.

As we began to descend, I could see the little village of A Ro to the south. Many clicks from there and we'd be home. It looked so easy by air. Laos, Cambodia, Vietnam—a hop, skip, and a jump.

"How we going to jump off this thing without him shooting us?" Quiet Voice shouted in my ear a few minutes later.

He had a point. If all three of us jumped off at the same time, he would just fly up to a comfortable height and blow us away. If Shotgun killed him before we jumped off, the helicopter would crash on top of us. This was a delicate moment.

It was as delicate as the pilot's touch on the Cobra as it hovered five feet from the safety of the ground. It was so delicate it confused even Shotgun, who dropped Spaghetti's shirt inside the bubble cockpit and jumped clear of the helicopter. By instinct we followed, which I immediately realized was a mistake.

The pilot swiveled his head to check on our positions on either side, then put the Cobra into a steep climb and began an extremely sharp turn to line us up within his sights. We stood numbly, even Shotgun, watching our death slowly turn to find us.

I think Quiet Voice was crying softly. I know I couldn't seem to get my breath, but what was worse was Shotgun shading his eyes with his hand so he could see the helicopter better. Had he given up after Spaghetti's death? Or was he showing us how to die with dignity?

"There it is," he said, pointing.

"Glad you pointed it out to us, Shotgun." I must admit at this point to a slight irritation that Shotgun's plan had gotten us this far and no further. I mean, what was the point?

"No, not the helicopter," Shotgun explained. "Look inside the cockpit." Shotgun's mouth was the thinnest I had ever seen it, which meant he thought this whole situation was hilarious.

Copying Shotgun—shading my eyes—I looked at the hovering craft, which seemed to be waffling side to side now. I tried but failed to see what Shotgun saw. All I could see was the stick shift between the pilot's legs.

Growing.

Getting taller.

No dick is that tall.

None.

Then its hood flared.

Cobra in a Cobra.

It's got a nice ring to it, doesn't it?

And that's the smartest thing I've ever seen.

I Win Shotgun's Respect

The cows were still shaken up from the burning helicopter, but that's understandable. The smell of a barbecuing pilot probably triggered a foreboding sense of their own fate. And they didn't calm down when Shotgun shot two of them for trying to stampede over us.

Still, I felt guilty about having left them ownerless earlier on our trip inward and decided to use the lessons I'd learned on a dry, worthless piece of land my father called home. These cows were fortunate because they could be worked on foot. Since each of us still had two of those, the cows responded well.

While Shotgun cut some steaks from the dead cows and plopped them on the helicopter fire, Quiet Voice and I gathered the strays and directed them towards south and home.

"Where did you learn to drive water buffaloes?" asked Quiet Voice, trying to imitate my cowboy noises as one particularly harsh bovine critic stepped on his toe.

"My old man used to smuggle Mexican cattle over the border to avoid the thirty-day quarantine at Juárez. He'd buy them for ten dollars from rustlers in Mexico and sell them for twenty dollars to fast-food restaurants.

"We tried to use horses but the cattle just bolted. They'd never seen a horse before. Same thing here. Just talk to them gently and they'll move on down the trail."

Shotgun came over, gnawing a piece of meat, and handed us the other two pieces. They tasted of fuel and metal and something else, but we were hungry.

"What you doing that for? We've got enough to worry about getting home," Shotgun said, watching the cattle meander down the trail.

It was my moment. "They can clear the trail ahead for us."

Shotgun studied me for a moment. His eyes almost focused on me as his lips grew thin. Grunting something unintelligible, he turned and followed our cows.

Bovine booby-trap seekers.

Four-legged minesweepers.

And three steak eaters.

We were down to our last ten cows when udder disaster overflew us. We were waiting for dark to fall before we crossed into Vietnam (we had just passed a well-known Cambodian village called Kompong Rau—you remember it) when a tremendous thunder began to build.

Looking eastward into Vietnam, we could see the sky growing black with helicopters. At the growing sound the cattle began pawing the ground and rolling their eyes like a herd before a stampede. But they, like

us, had nowhere to go. Quiet Voice and I watched in
awe. We could relate to what that poor enlisted German
soldier felt as Allied ships moved from the fog towards
the French beach in front of him. Even Shotgun gave
up.

"Well, shit. We gave it a good shot. If the pipeline
is that important, we don't stand a chance."

We stood there watching the waves of helicopters
coming towards us.

Getting closer.

Closer.

They were on top of us.

Then past us.

We watched them disappear deep into Cambodia.

A cow peed on the ground. I envied its nakedness
as I felt the wetness of my own pants. I glanced at Quiet
Voice. His pants were wet, too. That many helicopters
can trigger a physical response.

"Do you think they saw us?" Quiet Voice said.

"One did," Shotgun said, pointing.

A helicopter with the First Cavalry insignia painted
on its front, a black horse head on a yellow shield with
a diagonal black stripe running the length of the shield—a
nice target for a carefully aimed B-40 rocket—landed in
front of us, and a colonel hopped out and stood waiting.

He didn't kill us, so we waved and began driving
the cattle by him into Vietnam. We didn't want to hang
around in case he changed his mind.

Seeing we were not going to come over and visit,
he strode from the helicopter over to us. Okay, he
sprinted over to us. We still had time to take the
safeties off our weapons.

"Where the hell do you think you're going with
those cows?" he shouted.

We stopped.

"What business is it of his?" whispered Quiet Voice.

I walked over to him and told him we were on our way home.

He looked at our rags. He brushed some monkey shit off the tattered shoulder of my rotten jungle fatigues.

"I see you're a captain. Do those animals belong to Cambodian civilians?"

"No," I answered, "they belonged to Laotian civilians."

"What were you doing in Laos, Captain?"

"That's classified, sir."

"It involve cows?"

"In a way."

"What happened to your arm?"

"I was shot with an arrow."

"An arrow?"

"Yes, sir."

"Why?"

"Because the rubbers broke."

"I see. Do the rubbers involve these cows?"

"All but the yellow one. Shotgun still has it."

I think that if I had rolled my eyes and begun drooling at that moment, the colonel might have broken and run. Instead, I stood there quietly, which gave Shotgun and Quiet Voice time to move on down the trail with our food supply.

He took out a handkerchief and dabbed his forehead.

"It's been a long war, Captain."

"Yes, it has."

"It can play havoc with a man's sanity."

"It certainly does that, sir."

"Have you been in the bush long, Captain?"

"About four weeks, sir."

"You're a long way from Laos."

"Thank God."

"You couldn't walk that far in four weeks."

"We caught a ride on a Cobra."

"There are no passenger seats in a Cobra."

"On, sir, not in."

Mopping of forehead.

"How many passengers?"

"Four."

"But I see only three."

"Humans. That's correct, sir."

"Why didn't he give you a ride all the way?"

"Afraid of snakes."

"I see. Where is the pilot now?"

"Er...ah...Cooking at a barbecue."

"He's at a barbecue, cooking?"

I laughed at the colonel's sense of humor. I hadn't known colonels to have a sense of humor.

"What's so funny?"

I couldn't stop laughing. He waited to see if I would quit laughing; I didn't; he walked disappointedly back to his First Cavalry helicopter and lifted into the air.

I waved good-bye and followed Shotgun, Quiet Voice, and the cows back into Vietnam.

You Can't
Go Home
Again

Here's how the invasion of Cambodia was planned: a president with no field command experience, with the help of a German secretary of state, planned an invasion of Cambodia to look for COSVN, the mythical field headquarters of the North Vietnamese. Since this magical kingdom was somewhere in Cambodia, all available Americans were sent to Cambodia to find it.

The search for a communist grail, planned by the president, refined by the secretary of state, and implemented by the army high command.

Larry, Curly, and Moe.

If we had stayed any longer in Laos, we would have been caught between the bad boys in black helicopters and U.S. Army troops sweeping through Cambodia. Whoever had planned our demise had planned carefully. What that someone hadn't reckoned with was the capability and genius of Shotgun.

This had good and bad implications for Shotgun, Quiet Voice, and me.

The good implication was that we were still alive.

The bad implication was anyone that smart wasn't about to give up when we walked back into camp alive.

There was a growing need to sterilize the operation. Cut all leaks. Plug all holes. Neutralize any noise. Like the noise coming out of Quiet Voice's mouth.

"What do you mean, we have to stop?"

"Do you remember the last time we showed up at the camp and Spec. 7 Thompson met us at the gate?" I said, looking longingly down the dirt road that led to our camp.

Quiet Voice nodded his head.

"Maybe it would be better to approach it in broad daylight."

Quiet Voice accepted this better than I'd thought he would. Shotgun, who'd been listening to my idea, walked over and handed both of us the last of the meat from the barbecue.

"Tell you something, Captain. There's something strange about the village next to the camp." Shotgun motioned to the two of us to follow him to the Vam Co Tay River, the one that ran west of the camp.

"It's high tide." Shotgun waited for us to catch on.

We didn't.

"Where are their boats? You can see down this river for at least a mile and a half. You see any boats? They'd either be fishing now or returning from Moc Hoa. So where are they?"

He had a point. We walked back to the road and sat down beside it in the growing darkness. Shotgun didn't join us. He was staring towards the camp. "There's no lights in our gooks' hootch. We should be able to see the glow of their television from here."

"Maybe Spec. 7 Thompson didn't hook up a new one after he took their old one for the monitor," I suggested.

"Maybe." Shotgun sounded tense.

"Where are the cows?" Quiet Voice looked around in the gloom, trying to see where they'd gone.

Shotgun stood in the middle of the road. "The tracks point towards the camp. Let's follow them in."

"But, Shotgun," I protested, "it would be safer to wait until morning."

"They'll shoot the cows first if someone is watching the road. They'll think it's us. If we hear a shot, we drop and wait until morning."

It was a good plan.

That's what bothered me.

Ghost Town

The eerie thing about walking into an A camp in the middle of the night is the middle of the night. We shouldn't have walked right in but we did. Nobody tried to kill us. Nobody. We kept hearing the clack of the cows' hooves as they brushed against neighboring hooves and it sounded vaguely like an AK-47. The first few times we heard the sound, we hit the road on our stomachs. About the third time we did this, Shotgun stood and said, "I don't care if someone is shooting at us, my balls can't take this diving anymore."

So we followed the cows until we heard one of them brush the cowbell on the gate. The pastoral clang drove us to our stomachs again—all but Shotgun, who walked up to the gate.

"Where the hell is everybody?" he whispered.

"I don't know, Shotgun, but I'm tired. Let's sleep outside the gate and let the cows look around. If there is anyone still around, the cows will find them. Otherwise, we need the daylight to see what happened.''

Shotgun said into the darkness, ''What do you think, Quiet Voice?''

The only answer from Quiet Voice was quiet snoring. We joined him.

I awoke at noon the next day to the sound of cows munching contentedly on the grass inside the camp. For a moment I panicked: I thought I was in Texas. Then I saw the main gate, which hung crookedly on its broken hinges. It had been blasted open. The first triangle had been scattered across the flat area like a broken dirt clod pointing towards the middle triangle. The only part of our sign on the pole was the word ''normal.'' The rest of the slogan lay scattered around us.

I woke up Shotgun and Quiet Voice. We stood there wondering what to do until Shotgun motioned with his arm and we spread out in a crouching pattern. It was natural by now. We checked our counterparts' building first. Empty. No one home. Several of our Conexes were overturned and scattered. The steps leading down into our compound were covered with shrapnel from the blown door.

We walked to the opposite side of the outer berm and looked towards Thanh Tri Village. No village. No people. A few boats lay forlornly on the banks. Little pieces of tin lay scattered in the middle of a lonesome main street.

''What the hell happened?'' said Quiet Voice in an awed whisper. ''Where are the villagers? Why aren't there any bodies?''

''Where are Lieutenant Powell and Spec. 7 Thompson?'' There was a feeling growing inside me that hadn't been there before. Someone had taken my home and destroyed it. Someone had neutralized Lieutenant

Powell and Spec. 7 Thompson. This made it personal. There were many camps in Vietnam. Why pick on us?

Shotgun had wandered away from us out to the chopper pad. He picked up a large piece of webbing. We saw him kneel and begin to search the area on his hands and knees. Then he sat down and began to cook supper, which should have been breakfast, but since we hadn't eaten the night before, it looked like supper to me.

The cows, finding our camp to their liking, had wandered back out the gate and down to the river's edge. They began taking their fill of water, standing next to the abandoned boats.

I wandered over to Shotgun's little fire. He was using part of the gate for fuel.

"What now, Shotgun?" I said, squatting next to him.

"Where are the nearest tiger cages?"

Tiger cages? What made Shotgun think about tiger cages?

"Doesn't Moc Hoa have some old French ones?" Quiet Voice said, walking over to the two of us.

We weren't talking about zoo places for large kitties here. Go down into your basement and put five dog runs on each side, with a hall running down the middle. You know what a dog run is. It's a fenced place where dogs can exercise. Now, instead of wire walls separating the dog runs, put thick concrete. Don't make the walls too high—about five feet is adequate. Don't make the runs too wide—three feet will do. Don't make them too long—five feet is standard.

Now, don't put dogs in them.

Put human beings there. These things aren't good enough for dogs.

Since there are no doors at the end of the dog run,

you have to get in from the top of the cage. To keep humans in, heavy steel wire is laid over the top of all ten runs and the hall. A trapdoor is cut in the wire above each tiger cage. The door is opened to lower a human being into his run. Rarely does the human being come out. There is a little slit in the cage facing outward into the hall. It is pushed open to allow bread and water, if they're available, and an occasional spider to enter the darkened room. Sometimes, if you're really lucky, there's a single light bulb or two at either end of the hall so you can see the insects with the best protein and make a sandwich.

Since the top of the tiger cages is where the guards walk, the French guards began the tradition of just peeing or spitting on the prisoners rather than leaving their posts. That tradition had carried over to the Vietnamese.

And Shotgun was wondering where the nearest tiger cages were.

Shotgun bent forward to spread the coals on the fire.

"First we eat some steak, then we rest here for the day. Then we go to Moc Hoa and get Powell and Thompson."

Quiet Voice and I looked at each other. This tragedy on top of everything else was too much for Shotgun. It was time to admit he had gone crazy.

"Shotgun," I said, as gently as possible, "it's obvious the camp has been overrun and the villagers killed or captured in retaliation for the toleration of our camp, and Thompson and Powell are dead. Besides, where's this steak you're talking about?"

Boom!

Cow goes over the moon.

Shotgun laughed to see such a sight.

Quiet Voice and I quit shitting soon.

"What the hell was that?" I asked, picking myself up off the ground.

Shotgun placed a canteen cup full of dirty river water on the fire to boil. "I suspect one of the cows bumped one of those boats on shore."

"They're booby-trapped?" Quiet Voice ducked as a piece of cow thwapped the ground next to him.

Shotgun got up, walked over to the piece of cow—which turned out to be a hip and leg—dragged it over to the fire, and began cutting strips of meat off it to place on the coals. "They're all booby-trapped. They knew we'd need a boat to go to Moc Hoa if we wanted to get there quickly."

Why would we need a boat to get to Moc Hoa? I was beginning to worry about Shotgun.

The aroma of burning meat sickened me but my stomach said it would eat the meat, anyway. "Why would the NVA or VC worry about us going to Moc Hoa?"

Shotgun flipped one of the pieces over. "It wasn't the NVA or VC that emptied the camp or booby-trapped the boats."

"What do you mean, Shotgun?" I took off my rags and walked to the river's edge to clean them.

Shotgun tossed me the webbing he'd found earlier. The buckle made a little clink sound as it hit the dirt close to me.

"That's from one of those Chinook helicopters that's used for lifting a lot of weight. You know of any NVA with helicopters?"

I must admit that their command of the air was deficient.

"No," I said, "but if not the NVA, then who . . . ?"

He tossed another piece of webbing to me. There

was something with stripes tied to one end. I looked closely at it.

A tiger's tail. A little bloody, but definitely a tiger's tail. The nearest tigers were in Laos.

"The bastards left us a clue. Real cute. The Hawaiian shirts are sterilizing this mission. Saw their footprints around the chopper pad. Unless old Charlie is wearing sneakers, this enemy spoke English."

"Why didn't they just kill us here?" I tossed the tail back to Shotgun.

"They couldn't afford to wait. They didn't know how long it would take us to get back. So they just left us a clue to tell us where they're waiting with Lieutenant Powell and Spec. 7 Thompson."

"How do you know they're not already dead?" Quiet Voice curled up next to the fire and stared up at Shotgun.

Shotgun paused between gnaws on a large piece of meat. Squatting there, he reminded me of a caveman enjoying a lull between battles with the elements.

Thank God we're more advanced than that, I thought, as I picked a leech off my nuts.

Shotgun began to twirl the tiger tail around and around his arm. "They're not dead, they're bait." Then he gave an evil grin. It was the first time I'd ever seen him smile. "And we're the tigers coming into the trap."

"So that's why you asked about the tiger cages." Then I thought about walking all the way to Moc Hoa. Twenty miles isn't far unless you've walked from Laos. I glanced at the footwear on all of us. Our jungle boots were now down to jungle retreads.

"Quiet Voice, go into the village and see if you can find any clothing," Shotgun said. "We need to disguise ourselves for the trip. Captain, see if you can find any LAWs. We'll need those." Shotgun stretched and looked around.

Why would we need a light anti-tank weapon, I wondered as I watched Quiet Voice walk to the village. Were Lieutenant Powell and Spec. 7 Thompson that well guarded?

Shotgun stood up. "I'll find us some transportation. We'll follow the banks of the river to Moc Hoa."

Quiet Voice came back with clothes, I found three LAWs, and Shotgun brought back some fresh bamboo shoots.

I must have looked confused as Shotgun spread out the bamboo shoots away from our fire.

"It's for our transportation," he said by way of explanation as he walked past me back to the fire.

I looked at the bamboo shoots but said nothing.

We sat looking into the fire long into the night.

"Shotgun," I finally said, "if all the boats are booby-trapped, how are we going to get to Moc Hoa?"

He looked around into the night. "There's one thing a Chinook can't lift, and it's around here somewhere."

It was sad to see Shotgun start to slip. "Shotgun," I reminded him, "the jeep was blown up a long time ago."

"I know that! God, Captain, you're really starting to go."

"Did the CIA kill all of our mercenaries and the villagers?" Quiet Voice said from his fetal position.

Shotgun shook his head. "Didn't have to. Just offered them more money and relocated them to some other camp. Their loyalty is not the best. As for the villagers, they went to live with relatives or friends in some other town until we leave, then they'll come back. They've been doing it for years."

He sat there quietly for a while, and just before I fell asleep, I thought I heard him say, "Fucking war. There was a time when I liked being a soldier. It was bloody, sure, but it meant something. Now we're just janitors. Some damn politician or colonel makes a mess and we get to sweep it under the rug. We're janitors. Nothing else."

Like I said, I thought I heard Shotgun say that, but it seems like an awfully long speech for him. So it was probably just a dream.

On the Road
to Moc Hoa

Moc Hoa. The very name conjures up visions of mystery, intrigue, and malaria. Let me describe the town. Take the fort in *Gunga Din* with Cary Grant, add the lowlifes in *The Good, the Bad, and the Ugly*, throw Mike Fink and his River Pirates in for flavor, thicken with the smell of raw sewage and tidal flats, and bake well under a hot bitch of a sun and you have Moc Hoa.

Lucky for us Shotgun caught our EPC.

EPC?

Elephant personnel carrier.

Look, quite laughing. It's carrying us, we're army, we're personnel. So quit laughing. It can cross rivers, doesn't use much fuel, and affords us a 360-degree view of the land. Just because it travels at five miles per hour does not mean you have to stand there and laugh.

"Aren't elephants supposed to have long memories?" asked Quiet Voice, trying to adjust himself on the wide back. I could feel those little black wiry hairs pricking through my jungle fatigues and into my balls. It was like riding a giant Brillo pad with fleas. However, we were ten miles closer to Moc Hoa.

"She was looking the other way at the time of the explosion," said Shotgun. "If you don't say anything, she won't know it."

We had been working our way down towards Moc Hoa from the camp, using the banks of the river and the banks of the rice paddies. Shotgun front, Quiet Voice middle, and I in the rear.

Tourists.

A few farmers shook angry sticks at us for crushing a rice paddy or two; now, I'm no expert on elephants, but this one seemed a regular ballerina on those thin trails that led around the rice fields.

Shotgun hasn't said much. He just keeps muttering and saying things like, "At the rate we're going, they'll kill Thompson and Powell, end this war, and start another one before we get there."

He keeps kicking the elephant to try to hurry her up.

I wish he wouldn't do that. To keep him from abusing our EPC further I engage him in conversation. "Shotgun, what about Colonel Basshore? How does he fit in all this?"

He stops kicking. Good. "I don't know. If he's following orders, then he's an idiot. If he's in with them, then he's dead."

"Shotgun, you're not going to kill another colonel, are you?" Quiet Voice asks. He's spread-eagled on the elephant, which is forcing me closer to the tail.

"Don't have to. I'll just tell him what happened to us—talk about the pipeline, the drugs, and the CIA—

and the Hawaiian shirts will kill him to plug the leaks. Besides, we owe it to Subervich and Spaghetti. You know, there's a bond.''

Shotgun is getting to be a regular chatterbox. And what's this about a bond? Shotgun, Quiet Voice, and I? Linked forever? I start kicking the elephant to get my mind off the thought. She shifts to high gear: six miles per hour.

A lone sampan passes us. The long, narrow boat, driven by a farmer on his way back home from Moc Hoa, is filled with rice sacks and food. The farmer, surprised, turns and stares. In turning, he pulls the rudder around and runs up onshore, beaching the boat. Shotgun shoots him. Sudden movement and all that.

The elephant stampedes. Shotgun lurches forward. We bounce up and down, striving to keep from falling. I stare down at the pounding four tons of toes. The thought of slipping under those feet keeps me up.

''This is more like it!'' Shotgun shouts.

I try to answer him, but I keep getting the breath knocked out of me on the way down. Quiet Voice has shifted to the side and is hanging on to my leg. I reach down and grab him by the belt and pull him back up onto the elephant. While I'm doing that, he drops one of the LAWs but two are left. I look at Quiet Voice. He looks at me. He's turned around backwards.

''Make sure he doesn't drop the other LAWs!'' shouts Shotgun.

I still don't know why we're carrying the LAWs. Why will we need these things at Moc Hoa?

Not clear about LAWs, either? Well, your tax dollars bought 'em.

Let me refresh your memory about your purchase: a bazooka made from cardboard.

Does that help?

You hold the thing up to your shoulder, stretch it out to its full length, pop up the plastic sight, take off the safety, and fire it. After the bazooka rocket fires, you throw away the cardboard tube and get another one. The cardboard doesn't work when it's wet, which means you can't depend on the weapon in Vietnam. That's why we have three of them.

Had three of them.

The elephant hits the river that separates us from Moc Hoa. Can elephants swim? This one can. I am hanging on to its thick broom of a tail, Shotgun has an ear, Quiet Voice has nothing. He starts to float away but holds one LAW out of the water. Shotgun grabs it.

"Don't let it get wet!"

I watch the other LAW float down the mighty Mekong.

Quiet Voice keeps a death grip on the last LAW, knowing Shotgun won't let go. That saves him from being swept way. I am impressed with Quiet Voice's ingenuity. It rivals Spec. 7 Thompson's. Near-death experiences can do wonders for one's IQ.

The elephant impacts the opposite shore. The mud slows it down, allowing all three of us to get back on top. It plods up out of the mud like a great frog, trumpeting its anger at these little things that keep fucking with its life.

After the first Moc Hoa resident is stomped to death, the rest scatter and the dirt street in front of us is empty of people.

High noon.

At the far end of the street is the old French fort, now the headquarters for Colonel Basshore, formerly the headquarters for Black, the now-deceased colonel.

"Give me the LAW."

Shotgun jerks the weapon out of Quiet Voice's

death grip and aims it down the street towards the large wooden doors of the fort.

The elephant is standing, trembling, in the middle of the street, trying to get its breath.

"Shotgun?" I venture a small question.

"What?" he says angrily, trying to pry up the plastic sights.

"If the elephant panicked from you killing a farmer with a grenade launcher, what's it going to do when you fire a rocket?"

"I don't care what it does. It got us here and that's its mission." Shotgun aims carefully down the barrel, resting his cheek on the wet cardboard.

Quiet Voice turns to me and says, "Don't these things have backblasts when fired?"

I shake my head confidently. "Since it's wet, it probably won't fire."

We crouch low on the elephant's back anyway.

Shotgun squeezes the trigger.

Kaboom!

The elephant goes berserk.

The wooden doors of the fort explode inward.

That's what happens when the LAW is in town.

Shoot-out at the Moc Hoa Corral

Shotgun always liked to say, "If you're going to be stupid, you've got to be tough."

Stupid was shooting a LAW from the back of an elephant.

Tough was hanging on to a maddened, trumpeting beast as it thundered past stunned guards, through the shattered wooden gates, and plowed headfirst into the sleeping quarters of Colonel Basshore, thereby caving in the walls.

Unfortunately, Colonel Basshore wasn't at home. If he'd been there, all that followed could have been avoided.

His hootch maid, the little girl whose father had died in the sapper attack on our A camp and who Shotgun had sent back to the B team for protection, was inside and caught one of the elephant's toes right in her back, which cracked her spine as neatly as Shotgun could have.

She didn't have time to scream. If you've got to die, there are worse ways than being squashed by an elephant.

Maybe.

There was a strange look on her face when the elephant burst through the wall. It was that of an exasperated housewife who's just finished cleaning a room when the male walks through in muddy shoes.

That look changed to one of puzzlement as she disappeared under the gray mass. Saved from the wire of our camp to be squashed by an elephant later? Did the Buddha have an answer to that?

The elephant, knocked to its knees by the collision with the wall, gave a low rumbling groan and began to collapse on its side. All that could be seen of the little girl was her feet inside some old boots a soldier had given her. The rest of her lay hidden under the massive body.

Shotgun kicked a leg over the elephant's head to the other side and leapt to the ground. Quiet Voice and I followed. He knelt at the feet of the little girl and reverently took off her boots. Quiet Voice and I watched quietly. He tied the boot strings together and threw the boots over his shoulder. Standing, he ripped the iron legs off the colonel's bed. Some men do not handle grief gracefully. Shotgun was one of them.

He threw us the metal rails he'd torn from the bed. "Put these in your shirts. We may need them later." That was all the elegy he gave the little girl. But he wasn't going to forget. He still had the boots over his shoulder.

We walked out of the room into the bright sunshine of the fort's courtyard. Across the way was Colonel Basshore's briefing-and-commo bunker. The little boots swayed back and forth as Shotgun walked towards the bunker.

"That's far enough! Lay down your weapons. Resistance is useless!" Colonel Basshore's voice boomed from a loudspeaker mounted on a small pole in front of the sandbagged cement bunker. A group of the colonel's men filed quietly out and stood to the side of the entrance. Their guns were pointed at us and some looked as tough as Shotgun.

We looked at Shotgun. His lips were growing thin. What the hell was so funny?

And he began to tell the tale of Laos and Subervich and Spaghetti. His voice got louder as he described the pipeline, the volcano, and the poppies.

Some of the old-timers, realizing the danger Shotgun was putting them in, began drifting away.

Some of the old-timers who understood how the CIA and America plug leaks began to sprint out the splintered gates and down the dusty main street, away from the Tiresian voice of Shotgun, which by now had reached its full oratorical height.

Some of the old-timers who couldn't run because they were too shot up from World War II, Korea, and a thousand little hidden wars just stood there calmly with their hands over their ears and eyes. Hear no evil, see no . . .

Finally, the colonel came out alone, white and pale under the afternoon sun. His hands shook with righteous anger and pure fear as he pointed his .45-caliber officer pistol at us. At us: Right. Left. Up. Down. He was really nervous.

He looked at the boots Shotgun had over his shoulder. He looked past Shotgun at the damaged hootch and the large elephant. "Where's the girl?" he asked, shading his eyes and squinting.

Shotgun threw the boots at the feet of the colonel. "You were supposed to take care of her."

The colonel took an involuntary step backwards. "What did you want me to do? Put her in school? Send her abroad? My God! We can't interfere with the locals' lives like that. We're not their keepers, Shotgun."

"Then why are we over here interfering?" said Shotgun.

"To give them hope."

Shotgun looked back at the dying elephant and shook his head. "We've lost, Colonel. This isn't war. It's madness. That should be you under that elephant, not her. But things don't seem to go right in this country for some reason."

"Be logical, Shotgun. You can't beat all of us."

"There is no logic, Colonel, without moral absolutes to build on."

Quiet Voice tapped me on the shoulder. "What'd he mean?"

I shrugged my shoulders. "Beats me."

"Shotgun, your team is guilty of destroying government property and murdering a little girl. But I've called the necessary people to handle this." The colonel smiled at us, and I felt a cold chill run down my spine in the hot sun.

The colonel aimed his pistol at Shotgun. "They know you're here, Shotgun."

"They can't take the chance of leaving you and your men here alone, Colonel. They'll suspect I told you about the drugs and the pipeline and the airfield." It was clever how Shotgun got in his little advertisement.

"I'll lie."

That part would be easy for Colonel Basshore.

Shotgun shook his head. "If you lie, all the others that heard the story will have to tell the same lie. You can't get them to do that, Colonel."

The colonel blinked nervously in the sun and

licked his lips. "So what do you want me to do, Shotgun?"

Shotgun placed his M-79 on the ground. "Arrest us."

Quiet Voice looked at me. "What did he say?"

"Give up," I whispered.

"Where's his mind?" said Quiet Voice. "How come we came all this way just to let them lock us up? What's Shotgun up to?"

I didn't have an answer for him.

The colonel couldn't believe his stroke of good luck.

"Shotgun. I arrest you and your men for the destruction of government property and the premeditated murder of an Oriental. Is this what you want, Shotgun?"

Shotgun nodded.

We glanced at Shotgun. Premeditated? How could that be? None of us knew how to drive an elephant.

"It doesn't matter," said Shotgun. "I've been guilty of them all at one time or another during my lifetime. Take me to the tiger cages."

Whoa! Tiger cages?

I glanced over at the windowless, square one-story building set apart from the other buildings of the compound. Its gray walls were free of plants and dirt, as if even they didn't want to be associated with what went on inside.

As the colonel and his men led us to the compound, I heard Quiet Voice ask one of them, "How come it's away from the other buildings?"

"If we were close, we couldn't sleep at night because of the screams. This way we can get our beauty rest," the soldier said, chuckling at his own remarks.

I didn't think it was so funny.

"How come there's a roof over them now?" Quiet Voice had a point. When the French had built the tiger cages, they had dug a large hole in the ground and built ten cages, five on each side with a hallway down the middle. They had covered the whole thing with heavy galvanized steel wire so they could walk on top of the cages and the hall. Inside the hall were usually a guard and a specialized individual who extracted information from those in the cages. So why the building built over the cages?

The soldier prodded Quiet Voice in the ribs with his rifle. "You ask a lot of questions, you know that? We built the roof over the top because of army regulations . . ."

Good. At least somebody was checking on cruelty.

". . . concerning pollution."

We stopped and looked at him.

"The monsoon rains," he said, looking at us for understanding. "The rains fill up the cages, drowning the people in them, and we can't get information from them." He looked disappointed.

"What has that got to do with pollution?" I asked.

"All that old shit and pee flow out through the top and get into the water supply of the camp. Army health regs require us to keep the water clean as possible. So we had to build a roof."

"And clean out the cages?" Quiet Voice asked hopefully.

All of Colonel Basshore's men laughed at Quiet Voice's question.

Not a good sign.

He stopped talking as we approached a large steel door. In front, Basshore knocked twice and was answered with a similar knock from the inside. Then the door—I swear it did—squeaked slowly open.

The first thing we noticed was the smell.

It smelled like a giant hamster cage.

The next thing we noticed were the two individuals dressed in gray fatigues. They looked like diesel mechanics. There were brown stains on their shirts and pants. No soap could ever wash out those stains. Behind them was an iron gate and behind the gate were dirt stairs leading downward into a narrow dirt hall. There was no identifying mark—no insignia or names—on the guards' uniforms.

Shotgun looked at them.

"Project Phoenix?" he asked.

They nodded.

"You're Shotgun?" they asked.

Shotgun nodded.

"We've heard of you. This will be a challenge."

They turned and opened the gate and began leading us downward underneath the old French steel-wire roof and into the hall.

The two light bulbs at either end of the hall gave a low, sinister yellow light to this human hell.

We heard the elephant's last dying trumpeting from behind us in the daylight and then the sound of walls crumbling as the elephant kicked its feet for the last time. There was a large electrical popping sound as its massive legs ripped the generator's electrical wires from the colonel's sleeping quarters.

The generator stopped.

The two light bulbs in our hall went out.

It would be dark in the tiger cages.

This wasn't the way I had pictured it.

But in the dark, who cares?

Time
to Examine
Thoughts

You have a lot of time to think when you're alone
in the dark. You can't think when you can't lie down or
stand up. Since the walls were only five feet high to the
wire cage top and the cage was only five feet long, the
walls were too narrow to allow us to stand up comfortably and the cages too short to lie down in comfortably.
So I'd wedged myself between the walls about halfway
up. My floor seemed to move in the dark, so halfway up
the wall was better. I noticed that when I applied any
pressure to the walls, they seemed to give. The old
French concrete was soft from all the flooding.

I was trying to remember the Phoenix guys' rules.
They asked us to read them but it was dark, so they
repeated them from memory. "No talking until five
P.M. No talking after five-thirty P.M.; no talking while
eating. Food will be served at five-oh-one P.M. unless
you are caught talking prior to that."

The Phoenix Program was a program developed by the U.S. to destroy the communist infrastructure within South Vietnam. A Phoenix team would slip into villages at night with a local villager who would finger the hidden communist official. Of course the officials were always killed in their sleep, so they were never able to explain whether or not they were Communists.

The program had changed by 1969. The same people were going to the same villages but this time killing the loyal officials and leaving evidence that made it appear that the Communists were to blame. This way, it was thought, influenced by "gray" propaganda, the people would hate the Communists quicker because the good people were being killed by the "Communists," who were really the Phoenix people.

Understand?

So why were they running the tiger cages? It was my guess that they had to kill three more people and blame it on the Communists.

Hours passed after Colonel Basshore threw us into the cages. When the lights went out just after our arrival, Shotgun had told us to stay put or else someone would shoot somebody else by mistake. Then a light was brought to the colonel, who led us down to the end of the hall and to a ladder. Climbing the ladder first, he pushed open a wire door to the wire roof. We were motioned up, walked along the wire roof, and thrown into individual cells.

"Did you check them for weapons?" asked the bigger of the two Phoenix guards.

"Didn't have to," answered Colonel Basshore. "They gave them to us."

The guards laughed.

"I've still got a yellow rubber, and you'd better take the two metallic legs the other men have under their shirts," said Shotgun.

The guards laughed louder as they beat us with our own metal legs.

Was this Shotgun's idea of a practical joke?

"If you can find a way to use that rubber in the tiger cage, be our guest," one of the guards called out to Shotgun.

Things got quiet after the colonel left. I was in the second cage on one side of the hall. Next to me, I think, was Quiet Voice. In the cell at the far end on the same side of the hall was Shotgun. They hadn't put anyone on the other side. The guard, one of the Phoenix guys, walked past my cage whistling a small tune. The other one walked along the wire on top.

There was a strange noise coming from the end of the hall. To me, it sounded like a balloon stretching, but the darkness plays tricks on the imagination.

"Hey, guard," Shotgun whispered.

"That just cost you supper, Shotgun," said the guard, identifying his whereabouts in the darkened hall.

"What?" said Shotgun quietly

"I said—" There was a loud thwapp and the sound of a rock crushing a skull. There was a groan and then quietness again. The other guard, walking right above me, stopped.

"Bobby?" He squatted down, looking into the hall.

There was a groan at the far end. I could hear my guard walking down to the other end.

"Bobby?"

Thwapp. Then a thud as a body fell on the wire.

Then I heard the sound of a pair of hands breaking a neck. I crawled up to the top of my cage but all I could see was darkness.

Out of the darkness came Shotgun's voice. "These concrete walls are soft as hell. See if you can work on them and get down to my end."

I slid back down to the wetness at the bottom of my cage and slowly began to push against the rotten concrete with my boots as I braced myself against the wall. Next to me, I could hear Quiet Voice doing the same. It was our only chance. No one talked; the only sound was our breathing and scratching.

After what seemed like hours, my wall collapsed into Quiet Voice's cubicle. Together, we pushed down the walls in the cubicles between us and Shotgun.

I had never thought of my boots as being a horn of Jericho.

Or of Quiet Voice and myself as Joshua.

Later, much later, we rested. I had no idea what time it was or how long we had been working. My hands felt wet and I didn't know if they were bleeding or just sweating. I just sat alone in the dark, listening to my breathing.

And the cockroaches scurrying.

The rats rustling.

Spiders weaving.

Centipedes crawling.

I was one with a very small universe.

It occurred to me at that moment that a human being is a collection of a lot of defenseless parts hanging together for mutual protection. The brain is vulnerable to the elements. One small rock or elephant toe could smash it. So it makes a bargain with a skull, which in turn makes a bargain with nerves, which in turn make a bargain with muscles, which in turn make a bargain with blood vessels, which in turn make a bargain with a heart. All of them make a bargain with skeleton and skin. There are things within the human that are very much alone and scared.

When you're sitting in the dark, alone and scared, the fear does not come from the mind but from somewhere in the center of the chest. The thoughts come upward into the brain, not downward to the heart. It can't be proven, but at times like this, sitting in a tiger cage in the darkness, you know God is hiding somewhere deep inside of you because God is afraid of his own invention. You.

I felt alone.

We were going to die.

The darkness pressed downward.

God screamed from within.

I began to pray.

And from across the hall in the opposite row of tiger cages facing ours, my prayer was answered.

"Hey, Thompson. Is it five o'clock yet?"

There was a yawn and a small penlight came on in the cell across from me.

"Damn! Where are the lights? I'll get them working again. You promised me you'd read that last letter from your wife." It was Spec. 7 Thompson.

"I've read every one of them to you for the past five weeks! Christ's sake! Don't you know it rips my heart out when she writes how she goes down on those women each night after closing?" Lieutenant Powell didn't sound too happy.

"Yeah. But she did something to the redhead in the last letter, and I can't quite picture how she did that."

Lieutenant Powell screamed into the darkness. "Can't you see you're driving me crazy? *What does this madness all mean!*"

Shotgun answered from the void. "It means you keep your fucking mouth shut so we can get you guys out of here and leave this place. That's why I got us thrown in here in the first place. If you weren't here, it meant you were dead and I could leave without a guilty conscience. But since you're here, we've got to figure out a way to split.''

''Where are the guards, Shotgun?'' asked Lieutenant Powell.

''Dead.''

''How?'' asked Quiet Voice.

''Ever heard of David and Goliath?''

''This is no time for theology,'' said Powell.

So my prayers had been answered.

The answer was just a little complicated, that's all.

Thoughts
from Within

I hadn't known Lieutenant Powell long enough to see this side of his thoughts, but some people share things when they're out of control. Keep your head down because I don't want to know your thoughts, too.

Where are we?

If you'll stay down, I'll explain what's going on.

We'd already broken through to Shotgun's cubicle when we heard the sound of approaching helicopters.

"Now what?" said Quiet Voice, breathing heavily.

Shotgun whispered across the hall to Spec. 7 Thompson. "You got the wires ready?"

"No problem. Now if they'll just turn on the lights."

Great. The chopper is bringing in a million Hawaiian shirts to shoot us like dogs in these tiger cages and all Shotgun and Thompson can think about is getting the lights on so Lieutenant Powell can read his letter to everyone.

"If the lights go on, can't they see better into these holes to shoot us?" Quiet Voice sounds worried.

That's another disturbing point. I start to explain to Shotgun, but before I can, we hear the helicopter land. Then all is quiet. Above us in the courtyard we hear voices.

"Where are they?"

"This way." Colonel Basshore sounds almost apologetic. "Would you like me to let them out and have them brought here?"

"Too dangerous with Shotgun. We'll just shoot them where they are."

Fantastic. Shooting fish in a rain barrel comes to mind here.

The footsteps pause. "Aren't you going to give them a trial?" Colonel Basshore sounds worried.

Silence.

"Just asking. Follow me; they're over here."

The footsteps resume.

The door opens.

"Where the hell are the lights?"

"They tore up our wiring and shorted out our generator."

Good, I think. They won't come into the dark. We've got time. Time for what? Come on, Shotgun, the plan, tell us the plan.

"Thrailkill!"

"Yo."

"Fix the generator!"

"No problem."

Shotgun whispers, "Canada Thrailkill. Good man. Better than Thompson. Can fix anything electrical. Good with a knife in close quarters, too. They've sent the best."

He sounds proud.

The rest of those at the door climb to the top of our cages and wait for the generator. They're going to go cage by cage until they get to us and shoot downward through our huddled bodies. We've even gathered at the far end of the cages in a huddled mass so they can save ammunition.

Glad we pushed through the walls.

Great plan, Shotgun.

We hear their boots walking on top of the iron grate, spreading out over the cages.

"How many are there?" whispers Quiet Voice.

"Four, maybe five," answers Shotgun.

We hear the generator start.

"Told you he was good," says Shotgun.

It's still dark in here, though.

"Damn," says Colonel Basshore, "someone turned off the lights. I'll get them."

We hear him crawl down from the top of our cages and fumble in the dark for the light switch.

We tense.

I'm sure the bullets will bounce off.

We can feel the men above tense.

The lights come on.

We can see.

So can they.

They're still tense, even more so. Their bodies begin to shake, they're so tense. One Hawaiian shirt tries to open his hand, which is holding his weapon. Little curls of smoke are coming up around the hand holding the metallic stock of the Uzi.

In the cage across the hall we hear Thompson chortling, "It's working. God! If I'd only done this with my parents! Look at them fry. It's beautiful." In his cage we can see small wires attached to the top of the iron ceiling. There is only one light bulb working; The other is missing some wires.

Above us, the men give out a groan and fall, fixing us with a sunglassed stare. We could care less. We're alive.

"Open this door or I'll kill you where you stand," Shotgun says, waving a gun he took from one of the guards. He sounds all business when addressing a superior officer like Colonel Basshore, who stands at the switch on the wall directly across from Shotgun's cage. Etched on his frozen features is his distaste for yellow rubbers.

He meekly obeys. Shotgun shoves him backward and crosses the hall and lets Lieutenant Powell and Spec. 7 Thompson out of their cages.

Lieutenant Powell hugs Thompson. "How can I ever thank you?"

"Give me that last letter."

That's what friendship is all about.

We run to the end of the hall, Basshore bringing up the rear of our small band, Shotgun trailing him.

We burst out into the evening. The gray dusk is strangely muted and cool to our senses. We walk in a single line: Quiet Voice had the point, followed by Spec. 7 Thompson, me, Lieutenant Powell, Colonel Basshore, and Shotgun.

"Down!" Shotgun screams.

Quiet Voice, Thompson, and I hit the dirt. We hear Colonel Basshore hitting the dirt hard with his body from Shotgun's shove. The only one still standing is Lieutenant Powell.

"Now what?" said Lieutenant Powell, turning around towards Shotgun as Shotgun fires a burst at Canada Thrailkill, who has suddenly appeared from around the corner with a raised knife in his hand.

That's when I saw a side of Lieutenant Powell's thoughts dripping off my face and clothes. Brains are bluish gray in color. I'm sure part of what dripped off my clothes contained the words "Now what?" but I'm not sure where they were. I was only sure those two words had cost Lieutenant Powell his head. When Shotgun says "Down," it's better not to ask questions.

Life and Ink
Run Out at
the Same Time

After we shut off the generator, we packed the bodies in body bags and laid them out next to the chopper pad. Thompson wanted to turn the generator back on once we tore the cooked bodies from the roof of the tiger cages.

"Why?" asked Quiet Voice.

"I'm hungry. Cut up the elephant, put a few steaks up here, and we're set." I swear he was salivating when he said this.

Shotgun and Basshore have disappeared and haven't been seen for about three hours. It's pitch dark and we are working under the yellow lights of the compound. We get the final body to the pad and sit down. We are too tired to figure out what to do next.

"Too bad about Powell," says Thompson.

"I wonder if the mail pouch will have any of his letters?" Quiet Voice says, staring at me.

Spec. 7 Thompson leans forward and looks at me closely. "Yeah. If his wife doesn't know he's dead, she'll keep sending those letters. What do you say, Captain?"

"Anything to help the morale of the troops," I answer.

We all jump as three body bags land at our feet.

"Jesus Christ!" I shout at Shotgun, who has appeared out of the darkness. "You scared the hell out of us!"

He stands facing all of us, weapon leveled. "Get into the bags."

We stare at each other, but only for a moment. We climb into the bags. It's like crawling into your own coffin. But it beats having someone else put you there.

Like Shotgun.

After we're in, we hear Shotgun walking to each of our bags and attaching something to the top of each bag. Then we hear him lie down beside us and zip himself into his own bag.

The living and the dead lie side by side on the chopper pad. The difference is that they're not sweating and we are. It's stuffy inside the bags.

"Shotgun?" I venture.

"What?" comes the muffled reply.

"What if Colonel Basshore comes looking for us?"

"If I couldn't get out of a tiger cage, what makes you think he can?"

"I see."

"Shotgun?" It's Quiet Voice's bag.

"What?" Shotgun sounds like an angry parent from the bedroom telling the kids to quiet down. "I need some sleep here."

"Why the bags?"
"It's the quickest way to get to Saigon."
We're going home.
Next to me Shotgun snores.

Some Final Words

There was a lot of green on the runway at Tan Son Nhut, which meant a lot of soldiers. Maybe that's why the red, white, and blue of the flag-draped coffins stood out so much. There were soldiers in green jungle fatigues getting out of planes, soldiers in green jungle fatigues getting into planes, soldiers covered with green army blankets carried into planes, green trucks, green trailers, green helicopters, and green baggage carriers carrying the red, white, and blue coffins to the gaping hold of a large troop transport.

There the four of us stood: Spec. 7 Thompson, a scarecrow with brains; Quiet Voice, a tin man with a heart; Shotgun, a not-so-cowardly lion; and I, a nervous Dorothy not quite believing he was really going home.

I glanced at the body bags we held, each bag tucked neatly under an arm. I also glanced at the chains on our feet and hands.

What were we doing in chains?

Let's go back to the body bags on the chopper pad at Moc Hoa.

The sound of the incoming choppers woke me up. I heard Shotgun wake up, too.

"Everybody stiffen up!" he ordered.

"Why?" asked Quiet Voice.

" 'Cause the dead ones are. We've been waiting all night."

The medivac arrived, and we were pitched onto what felt like an unceremonious pile of bodies in the helicopter.

I heard the door gunner tell the pilot, "Let's get the hell out of here. Whatever killed this many people might still be around."

How true, how true.

Once back at the body-processing unit in Saigon, we lay stiff until silence settled on us. Unzipping our bags quietly, we stood up and looked around. There were many bags all around us in what looked like an empty airplane hangar.

Shotgun began unzipping other bags quickly.

"Shotgun! What the hell are you doing?" I asked.

He looked inside one body bag and shook his head and then went to another. "This one will do. Quiet Voice! Get over here and stand so I'll remember which one is which."

Quiet Voice quietly obeyed.

He found two more and had each of us stand over a bag. He ran back to our empty bags and tore off our identification tags and tied them to the dismembered parts within the bags we were standing over.

He walked back, rolled up the empty body bags, and handed each of us one.

His lips tightened into a thin line. "Had to find the

bags without any heads. Fortunately, that wasn't too hard. Now, when the Hawaiian shirts come to check on us, they'll think we're dead.''

''You will be if you move a muscle.''

We all froze. A lone figure carrying an M-16 walked towards us from the far end of the hangar. We breathed easier. At least it wasn't a Hawaiian shirt.

''My name is Colonel Hastings and I'm in charge of all this,'' he said, sweeping one arm wide, keeping the other aiming the rifle at us.

''And you're the first that ever got out of the bags.'' He said this with a note of wonder in his voice. With his unoccupied hand, he reached into the side pocket of his jungle shirt and pulled out a bottle.

Unscrewing the top with his teeth, he took a swig from the bottle and tossed it to Shotgun. ''Now, what're you boys doing here?''

Shotgun explained everything. It wasn't the truth, but it sure sounded good.

For a long while we passed the bottle around in silence. The bags filling the great hangar seemed to strain to hear our story. I knew each one of the soldiers in the bags had been just like us once—alive and happy.

Finally the colonel said, ''My orders are to process the bodies and send them home.'' He studied each of us carefully. ''You look processed to me. Now, carry the bags under your arms so my men will know you're dead.''

We looked at each other.

''Since my men might be a little nervous about talking to dead people, I'm going to put you in chains so they'll feel in control.''

The colonel stared at Shotgun long and hard. ''You no longer exist, you know. Basshore is dead by now. They'll check here and I'll show them the bags. You're officially dead and out of the army.''

For a moment Shotgun seemed stunned—perhaps he was surprised that someone of colonel rank was giving us a fair shake—then he looked around at all the body bags.

"Good," was all he said.

The chains were uncomfortable. They were the kind that wrap around the waist and have a strand or two that clink downward to connect with ankle cuffs. And a strand or two that manacled our hands.

We were waiting for the plane to be loaded with the coffins so we could take our places in those little web seats that are always in the tail section of transport planes. The only problem is, you can't sit down until the crew chief hits a button that closes the rear section, because there's no floor if the door remains open.

A comforting thought if you're flying at thirty thousand feet and the tail door pops open.

A comforting thought if you're watching the take-off through your legs by looking through the large crack where the door doesn't fit as tight as it should and the trees get smaller as you gain altitude but then get larger as you plummet towards the earth due to an engine malfunction.

A real comforting thought if the plane has to ditch in the Pacific and you—in chains—have to tread water.

We couldn't wait to get on board.

Once we got home, the theory went, since we didn't exist anymore, the government would allow us to leave uncontested.

Every now and then, one of the body-processing officers would come by, check our tags, look at the body bags under our arms, shake his head, and walk on. They didn't talk to us or look at us.

Dead weight has that effect on people.

We were guarded against attack from Hawaiian

shirts by several burly Hoa Haos summoned mysteriously by Shotgun. They had appeared suddenly while we were waiting to board the plane, which had TIGER AIRLINES spelled out along the side. It made me think of tiger cages. Later, I read that Lyndon and Lady Bird owned stock in that airline. Of course that had nothing to do with its contract to fly "our dead boys home."

Another comforting thought.

"Something has to be said," said Shotgun.

"About what?" said Quiet Voice.

"Subervich, Spaghetti, and Powell." Shotgun turned and looked at both of us. "We didn't have time to say anything for them. They need a service."

"Isn't it a little late to be thinking about a funeral service?" asked Quiet Voice.

A priest was sprinkling water on one of the caskets and kissing a piece of cloth. Shotgun shuffled over to him and tapped him on the lower back, since he couldn't raise his manacled hands to tap him on the shoulder.

The priest turned. We couldn't hear what they were saying because of the engine noise, but we saw the priest shake his head. Shotgun's hands were a little below waist level, otherwise he would have grabbed the priest by his collar. Where he did grab him convinced the priest to nod.

Shotgun pointed to three coffins and seemed to say, "These will do."

Shotgun motioned to us to join him around the coffins. Our guards stayed behind, believing the ghosts of the dead still lingered close by. They were probably right. And if they were, Vietnam is one of the most populated countries on earth.

The priest raised his arms in prayer and began saying the usual words, like "dust to dust," and "God works in mysterious ways," and "man must suffer." Quiet Voice and I bowed our heads. Shotgun just scowled at the priest.

I think it was around the time the priest said that "we shouldn't question God's plan" that his voice got higher, causing us to look up from our prayerful position. Shotgun had grabbed him in the same place and was looking at him real close.

The priest glanced at us for help but we only shrugged our shoulders and showed him our chains. He was on his own. He studied Shotgun's face and saw the effect of wars and more wars; he saw man's inhumanity to man; the scars from old shrapnel and dirt permanently etched in Shotgun's face; he saw all this and made up his mind to give the sermon he'd always wanted to give.

Shotgun didn't relax his grip. Therefore, you must imagine that you are hearing this speech in falsetto.

The priest cleared his throat. "There are no new sources for molecules in the universe. What is here was here when God created it all. No new protons, electrons, or neutrons. We are told by Mr. Einstein that energy cannot be destroyed. So where is..."

He paused here and looked at Shotgun, who replied, "Sergeants Wilson and Subervich and Lieutenant Powell."

"...Sergeants Wilson, Subervich, and Powell? Where are they now? Heaven? Hell?" The priest took a deep breath. He was about to plunge into the unknown. Shotgun relaxed his grip. "If they were energy, they, too, can't be destroyed. They are standing in line, gentlemen, or rather their molecules are, standing in the door, waiting for the sign from the Jumpmaster to leap into the chaotic maelstrom of the universe. Perhaps to be assigned to the making of a new flower, a new planet, a new star, a new soldier, or a new war.''

The priest's eyes were wide, his face flushed, and his breathing heavy. He was about to make a point.

''Since there are infinite choices of random patterns in the chaos, it means''—he paused for dramatic effect, then shouted above the roar of the engines—''it means we will do this all again, over and over and over.''

Shotgun wiped a tear from his eye by bending his head forward and rubbing it on the priest's back. ''Well said, Padre, well said. Now, that is comforting.''

Comforting?

To repeat Vietnam over and over?

It's all one big fucking cosmic joke?

The universe ruled by Bozo the clown?

The final trumpet is really Clarabelle's horn?

All this is an advertisement for itself?

I can't wait to fit right back in.

Change the channel, Subervich, wherever you are, change the channel.

It's Howdy Doody time!

Honk-honk.

Time to End the Show

Fighting soldiers from the sky—
These are men who jump and die—
One hundred men will test today—
But only three wear the Green Beret.
　　　—from "Ballad of the Green Beret"
　　　　　M. Sgt. **Barry Sadler,** Special
　　　　　Forces
　　　　　(Dead of alcohol poisoning
　　　　　somewhere in South America)

The plane trip took twenty years. That's a long time for an airplane ride—even one from Vietnam.

I remember landing with Shotgun, Quiet Voice, and Spec. 7 Thompson in Seattle. We walked out with

all the coffins and were immediately told to halt while a
U.S. Customs German shepherd sniffed our nuts, along
with the coffins, to make sure no drugs had been
smuggled home by some poor enlisted stiff.

I thought about Air America.

The dog hit my crotch with his searching nose.

I smiled. It should have been trained to sniff my
thoughts.

I looked down at my tattered uniform and noticed
that the dog had a cold or one hell of a runny nose. He
started sneezing heavily. He mustn't have liked Vietnamese
dirt.

I didn't either.

Welcome home, boys.

I saw Shotgun take one last look at us and then he
saluted me. He'd never done that in Vietnam. "It could
cost you your life," he told me. "They'd know which
one to shoot."

I couldn't return his salute right away because of
the tears in my eyes. When I did return it, and my eyes
had cleared, he was gone.

"What'll we do now?" asked Quiet Voice.

Spec. 7 Thompson was looking at a brochure that
he'd picked off the runway. "The future is VCR. No
more channels to change!"

He wandered away from us glassy-eyed.

I left Quiet Voice standing on the runway still
asking questions. Outside the airport, I got drunk in one
of those bars set up for relieving returning vets of their
leave money. It was the least my country could do. As I
staggered back to the airport, three cops descended on
me. They were concerned about my creative walk
across the street on all fours. The "vill" was definitely
hostile. They certainly had things organized. I still have

the jaywalking ticket, Seattle. It looks a lot like ticker tape if you look at it just right.

I got back on the airplane and got off at the University of Texas in El Paso in 1972. The landing was announced by a professor who popped a Mickey Mouse balloon in my English class, which was her way of telling us she was playing no more Mickey Mouse games with our test results.

I had my back turned when she did that.

After I got up off the floor, I told her to shove the balloon up her ass. I didn't pass her course.

That's okay. She wouldn't want to pass mine.

While I waited outside a psychology class, the girl whose father was an FBI agent and who'd rolled up inside a blanket with me the night before I left for the army walked by. She was holding on to one of my professors from another time and telling him what she was going to do for him that night and I wanted to tell her something but I couldn't remember her name and I didn't know what it was I wanted to say and they walked on and I wanted to feel something but there was nothing when I looked inside so I left, knowing I'd learned too much from a different school. UTEP had nothing for me.

I began coming back to America in 1977 when the doctor started talking about insertions.

"Insertion" is not a good word. I'd heard it used once a long time before by a crazy colonel in a tiny country the shape of an arthritic Florida. It's a fearful word.

Insertions always took something away. I left pieces of that something in places with strange-sounding names, like plaine des Jarres, Plain of Reeds, Moc Hoa, Thanh Tri, A Ro, and Parrot's Beak. Now, looking at my small two-year-old son lying in the hospital bed, I realized another piece was being taken from me.

"We inserted the scalpel here and here to find the testicles and bring them down into the sac. The sac itself had to be rebuilt because there wasn't enough room for the testicles to grow. Unfortunately, the left testicle's blood supply had been cut off at birth by a herniated intestine and it had to be removed. We don't know if your son is going to be sterile; we'll have to wait until puberty to see.

"There is some speculation in medical journals that this type of problem occurs more frequently in Vietnam vets who've been exposed to Agent Orange. If you were exposed to Agent Orange, we have a questionnaire developed by the Veterans' Administration we'd like you to fill out, please."

I was aware that the doctor was watching my hands grip the iron rail that held my son's leg. The hands were white and the veins prominent. The bed began to shake, not large shakes, which might cause more pain, but a small, steady one like a scream translated through metal. I wanted to apologize to the doctor for my hands but there was nothing I could do but wait for the red tide in front of my eyes to pass.

I was sure the doctor was saying something but I heard nothing except the din of rotor blades changing pitch for final approaches.

And I saw a white jungle with animals pointing their feet towards the sky.

Were we two more KIAs? Had Agent Orange killed my son and me?

Sorry, son. No war stories for you. Your scars say you're a veteran along with me.

I think it was when I shot holes in my library walls that psychological counseling was suggested. I'd been reading Sherlock Holmes and wanted to see if I could spell "VR" the way he did when he shot the initials of Queen Victoria (Victoria Regina) into the wall of his Baker Street flat.

My wife called the cops. The judge suggested counseling or jail. Counseling sounded better. It helped.

There were a lot of guys in that counseling group who'd been on the 'Nam plane for as long as I had. One was Leon Hanson.

Leon Hanson could throw his leg farther than any man I know. Of course, Dr. Timothy Patton couldn't possibly have known this when he began supervising a small Vietnam support group at the Blue Mountain Mental Rehabilitation, Eating Disorders, and Spiritual Sauna Bathing Clinic, one of the many clinics begun by enterprising and caring young psychologists who realized there was money to be made in our nightmares.

Since we wouldn't go to the VA, they decided to come to us. More specifically, they decided to go to the employers and local law enforcement agencies and ask them questions:

Has anyone gone berserk over small slights, like a poor job evaluation, and threatened to blow up the whole business?

And tear the balls/breast off said evaluators?

And/or carried out those threats?

Driven a car—his or stolen—into the front office?

Does his job application list several hundred jobs that terminated over trivialities?

Does he respond to chiding over a smudged paper or an unclean desk by saying, "It's no big fucking deal"?

On Saturday nights, does he often shoot holes in his mobile trailer, screaming at the stars?

Does he curl up in a fetal position and sleep for two years?

Do the wife and kids pack up and wave bye-bye and drive off in the station wagon because he refuses to cut the grass because if he did, it would give his neighbors a clear field of fire?

Then, employer/policeman/family member, you may have a veteran suffering from posttraumatic stress syndrome, and the government will pay the Employee Assistance Program costs to have the employee sent to a Vietnam veterans' support group.

And we sat there and talked. There were anorexia groups next door and kleptomania groups down the hall, so we felt at home. Dr. Patton would talk and we tried not to laugh. The FNG—fucking new guy—would try to use his schooling to show us how our emotions oscillated past meridian. It seems Vietnam caused unreasonably high levels of emotion and supplied depressive situations.

You could say that again, Doc.

Vietnam supplied unreasonably high levels of emotion and depressive situations, which caused the mental state to fluctuate past a meridian and set emotions to bouncing.

Really? Just because all of us would, upon walking into a cafe, for instance, try to figure out how to get out of there in case of a firefight didn't mean he was right. . . .

Just because we would daydream about killing . . .

Just because most of us quit jobs between November and March, when the clouds hung low on the mountains and it was miserable and wet . . .

Just because we'd be carrying on a normal conversation, then forget where we were . . .

. . . did not mean he was right.

Then he said, "You've got to forget about Vietnam."

And he smiled and leaned back in his office chair, which was in the circle but it had padding and we were sitting on folded chairs but, hey! *He understood us.* We had to forget Vietnam.

No problem.

Leon stood up.

He took his pants off,

Unbuckled his leg,

And began hopping towards Dr. Timothy Patton.

His arm held the leg high and his face was a complete blank, which was bad for Patton, who'd been trained to read faces. When he got to the arm of Dr. Patton's chair, he balanced with one hand while slowly bringing the leg down in repeated arches on Dr. Patton's head.

"You son of a bitch!" Leon screamed, which wasn't that unusual. Leon screamed those words all the time.

What *was* unusual was the sound a hollow leg makes hitting a psychologist over the head.

Thwwunk.

Thwwunk.

Chink, chink.

Thwwunk.

Thwwunk.

Chink, chink.

The chinking sounds were the leg-strap belts slapping against the side of the plastic leg.

"You son of a bitch! Tell me how I'm supposed to forget about Vietnam when I have to strap this fucking thing on every morning when I sit on the edge of my bed!"

Leon had a point. We waited for Dr. Timothy

Patton to respond, but instead he called the guards. As they were carrying Leon off, he raiscd his arm like a crippled Loki and threw that leg like a lightning bolt. He missed the doctor but caught the picture window perfectly. The outside air felt good in that office.

The counseling lasted for a year. Some of us made it. One started an Italian restaurant. His name was Iannuchi, so that was a good choice.

Another started a stolen-car ring. He's successful, too.

Another walked away still confused, looking, like Quiet Voice, for the why of it all.

I found it in a lecture given by one of the great generals of the war. A general is what happens when a colonel survives. I made sure I got there early enough to sit in the front row. I looked around for Shotgun and was relieved at seeing that he wasn't there. Generals deserve to die in bed. I sat next to the commanding general of our ground troops in Korea. He was tall, and a friend of the lecturer, who was surprisingly short. Mutt and Jeff. Both had bushy, thick eyebrows. Could this be the mark of leadership? They were both old and their hands shook. They looked human. On the other side of the Korean gentleman was the wife of the lecturing general. She introduced herself to me and asked if we had met somewhere. I looked familiar, she said.

I mentioned that I'd worked for her husband.

In a way that's true.

She smiled and said she remembered me.

I told her I remembered her.

She looked pleased.

Then he began to lecture.

Why didn't we cut the supply line of gasoline in Laos? was the question I couldn't wait to ask him. He was certain to have the right answer.

Clear it up.

Put it to rest.

Store it in the archives.

Wrong.

He showed us where Southeast Asia was located—Vietnam, Burma, China, the Philippines, and the Middle East. He talked about how Vietnam was doing our job and containing China. He talked about the irony of that. It wasn't lost on me.

Then he said that the reason for Vietnam was . . .

I waited.

Edge-of-the-seat time.

No one breathed at all.

Especially fifty-five thousand.

No talking, please.

Vietnam was fought to protect the natural resources found in Southeast Asia—oil and rubber.

There were no trumpets. No parting of the skies. People breathed again. But I was grateful. I wiped away a tear. Randy died for Exxon and Detroit. There was a reason. The great general knew why. America had to be made safe for the corporations, and Vietnam's going Communist threatened all that. It makes sense. Just ask Dr. Timothy Patton.

But reasons often sound so hollow.

Thwwunk.

Beached

Although it's 1992 and there's been another war, I feel like I just got home. The kid is doing fine. I think the nut is growing. Doc says it is, but I don't trust him.

Greatest news now would be an angry father calling me up and saying, "Your son of a bitch son got my daughter pregnant!"

Call me collect.

Spaghetti is on the Wall. I've seen his name.

They weren't going to put Subervich's up there.

No body. No name.

About a thousand letters later he's there, with a little star by his name. I can give you the panel and line if you want.

It was all I could do. It wasn't enough.

But it's something.

Quiet Voice? He's working for the IRS as a field agent. I can hear him now: "And this item here? What

about line 33 here? Do you really intend to claim
this?''

Spec. 7 Thompson is in Los Alamos.

God help us.

And Shotgun. Where is Shotgun?

I read an article in the paper the other day. Here is
what it said:

Vietnamese Restaurant Robbed

Mr. Hoang Ka, proprietor of Dragon's Tale, a
popular Vietnamese fine food restaurant at the
corner of University Boulevard and 6th Street
near the University of Minnesota campus was
robbed Thursday morning by a lone man at
gunpoint.

The patrons of the restaurant were tied
and blindfolded by strips of an American flag.
The police, calling this the third robbery in
the area by the ''flag bandit,'' are warning he
may strike again. All restaurants are cautioned
to be on the alert for an elderly man in jungle
fatigues. He was last seen leaving the restaurant in an old French Citroën.

Police traced him to a partially destroyed
gasoline station and found some supplies under a Temporarily Closed sign. Search of the
premises has halted while awaiting a team of
bomb specialists from Ft. Ord.

It's good to see Shotgun survived.

Me?

Sit here on the sand with me at Hunting Island

below Beaufort, South Carolina, and I'll tell you about something I left out.

My son is out there playing in the waves, riding something called a boogie board. He hisses down those waves at breakneck, foolhardy speed, heading towards shore. The surgery scars have faded to almost nothing. They're only noticeable because of his tan. Look at the shrapnel scars here on my arm. You didn't notice them, did you? They're almost forgotten, too. He and I have matching scars.

Hunting is a fine island. It's a state park, so there's little development. Those who want to be seen don't come here. They're over there on Fripps Island, the island to the right of where we're lying here on the beach. These condo commandoes spend "mini" vacations down here, whatever that is; as if making money and keeping it are more important than feeling the sun on your skin now, hearing the joy of your child now, watching a pelican wheel and dive now, feeling life now. There is no later.

That other island? The one beyond Fripps?

That's Parris Island. That's where they send sons to learn from a very old text. Like Shotgun, Quiet Voice, and Spec. 7 Thompson, they'll be trained as janitors to sweep up messes made by politicians, and they'll be paid by people like you and me. Before we write the check, let's make sure their janitorial help is needed. Above all, don't ever look down your wealthy noses at janitors again. They don't have much choice about the work they do.

I want to tell them about the pipeline in Vietnam but my words would be drowned out by the sound of the crashing waves. I think about Shotgun again. That's what I wanted to tell you about at the start, anyway.

Shotgun refused only one order in life. That's not a

bad record. Putting trust in authority figures, hoping
they know and do the right thing, requires a great deal
of courage and faith. Shotgun had courage. None of us
had faith.

Remember the little boy and his grandfather? Shotgun refused to kill them.

"No." That was the word he used.

I didn't ask again. His refusal was like the sun
refusing to come up.

The waves refusing to roll.

Fall leaves refusing to change.

The world shifted and we all knew it. I looked
around at Quiet Voice, Subervich, and Spaghetti, but
they wouldn't look at me. I felt like a driver on a side
road trying to break into a long car line; YOU know how
none of the motorists will look you in the eye, staring
straight ahead, pretending you don't exist?

I knew then they were not killers. They had killed
but they were not killers. There is a difference between
killing in combat and killing. Do you understand that? I
didn't understand that. Philosophy 101 doesn't cover
that particular issue.

What was even more surprising was the discovery
that I was a killer. I took out my Randall knife, wiping
the blade on my pants leg like an apology for the dirt.
My men didn't stop me. It had to be done. They knew. I
knew.

They drifted off to "provide cover" and I was
left alone with a frightened old man and a trembling
child.

Relax.

I'm not going to put you through my nightmare—
it's hard enough telling you this much—but afterwards,
as I cleaned the knife on the grass, I thought about my
daddy cleaning the first deer I killed. I cried then, too,

as his old barlow knife ripped into the beautiful skin and left nothing but silence for what once was.

I've often thought about why I killed them. It didn't hurt inside when I did it. There was no feeling at all.

That's the horrible part.

I suppose I'll go through life with this ache deep within that's not really treatable. I first became aware of the ache when my son was born. It got worse each year as he approached the approximate age of the little boy. The ache almost ripped my body apart when we visited a petting zoo and my little one picked up a stick and slapped an old milk cow on the rump. My wife laughed and gave him a hug. I got sick.

But the strange thing is, for every year my son has passed the age of the little child dead in Laos, the ache has diminished accordingly. Every time I give him a hug or tell him I love him, I can feel the ache receding. Maybe the mind that looks back and judges is a more mature mind than the one that made the decision in the first place.

We couldn't be here if we hadn't been there.

Maybe by loving my son I can make up for taking love away from another family.

Maybe.

I showed my son the Wall and all those names, and after a long silence, he looked at me and said, "Let's go home, Daddy. There's nothing more to do here."

So we did.